MADDOX'S *Truce*

USA TODAY BESTSELLING AUTHOR

HEATHER SLADE

Maddox's Truce
© 2018 Heather Slade

Second Edition

ISBN 13: 9798886490763

MORE FROM AUTHOR HEATHER SLADE

Table of Contents

1

If he weren't in someone else's house, Maddox would put his fist through a wall. He'd put up with Alex's shit for almost twenty years, and he was just about done.

He'd been done before, yet somehow, he always circled around and ended up right back where he was now.

Her latest? Offering to babysit her best friend Peyton's kids at his house. His house. Not hers. His. As far as kids went, they seemed okay, but Maddox never babysat anyone's kids, not even his niece, Spencer. His sister Skye never asked. She was too smart to consider leaving a child in his very incapable hands.

Alex had been avoiding him since this morning, when he'd tried to stop her from interfering with his brother's relationship with her best friend.

She ignored him, as usual. And she'd been right, as usual. He'd been trying to get Brodie to pull his head out of his ass and fix things with Peyton for days, and in two hours, Alex had managed what he couldn't.

Now Peyton and Brodie were reunited and about to leave for her house while Peyton's two sons were packing their stuff for a slumber party with Uncle Maddox.

That's what Alex had called him, and while it was likely Peyton and Brodie would be married sooner rather than later, especially given she was pregnant with Brodie's child, wasn't calling him the boys' uncle taking things too far?

Maddox followed Brodie and Peyton down the stairs and carried her bags to Brodie's truck.

Alex closed the door after Brodie helped Peyton inside, and rested her arm on the bottom of the open window. Maddox couldn't hear what she said to Peyton, but he could see her eyes fill with tears.

When Alex backed away from the truck, he was right behind her and wrapped his arms around her waist. They waved as Brodie drove away.

"We need to talk," he whispered.

When she tried to escape his hold, he tightened his arms.

"You're not goin' anywhere, Alex. We're gonna talk."

"No, we aren't, Maddox."

"What's this Uncle Maddox crap?"

"Seriously? It isn't going to kill you to do something nice for your brother, especially with all you put him through."

He let go and spun her around. "What did you say?"

"You heard me. You could've helped him, Maddox. Instead, you played the almighty omniscient, telling him he had to figure things out for himself. Meanwhile, my best friend was as heartbroken as Brodie was."

"If I had to do it over again, I wouldn't change the way I handled it."

"Of course not."

"You can't admit that if Brodie had gone in guns blazing, the way he planned to, he would've driven Peyton further away?"

"You could've told him how she felt."

"No, I couldn't have, because I don't know Peyton the way you do. You may say it was that simple, but you know damn well it wasn't."

"It doesn't matter. They're back together now, and her boys, who happen to be my godsons, are standing on the porch of their grandparents' house watching the guy whose house they're sleeping at tonight argue with their aunt.

"I'm honored to be their aunt, Maddox. They're amazing boys who are about to watch a shitstorm custody fight go down between their mother and a father they've never known. Do I want them to have a night away from all the crap that's been going on in their lives? You bet I do. I'm going to make this the best damn sleepover they've ever had. If you can't help me make that happen, at least stay out of the way and don't spoil it for them."

As much as he wanted to wring her neck, it was this fire in her he couldn't resist. She'd stand up for the defenseless, soothe the pain of those who hurt, and fiercely protect those she loved. There were times he wished she loved him, but more often, the idea that she might scared the living shit out of him.

When Alex walked over to where the boys waited, Maddox stayed where he was and watched her joke and laugh with them. She had a smile that never failed to knock him on his ass. It had since the first time he'd met her.

Her long brown, almost black, hair hung straight today, the ends just kissing the curve of her ass—another thing about her that never failed to knock him on his.

She was wearing jeans, rolled up far enough above her ankles to show off her hotter-than-shit, red suede boots with the three-inch heels. The cream-colored, sleeveless, silk and lace blouse she wore was long in the back, but short enough in the front that when she stretched, Maddox caught a glimpse of her tan belly. Her eyes, the same color as her hair, danced as she talked with the boys.

Maddox finally joined them on the porch. "Ready, guys?"

Jamison, Peyton's oldest son, was ten. His brother, Finn, was eight. When he and his brother Kade were their age, they had their own "best damn sleepovers"—ones Alex couldn't even imagine. They'd have fun; he'd make sure of it. The same kind of fun he and Kade used to have.

Before he was killed in Afghanistan on what was to be his final mission with Delta Force, Kade had dated the boys' mother. Maddox knew that, even though they welcomed Brodie's role in their mother's life, they still missed Kade. How could they not? He was the coolest guy who'd ever lived.

If Alex wanted them to have fun tonight, they sure as hell would. She might not, but they would.

Maddox loaded the boys' bags into his truck and told them to climb in the back seat of the big SUV.

"Ready?" He winked at Alex.

"What are you up to, Mad-man?"

"You'll see, Al. You wanted fun, right?"

—:—

Oh, Lord. What had she started?

It had always been this way with them. She'd challenge him, and then he'd step up and blow her away. Maddox Butler was the least boring man she'd ever met and, by far, the hottest. He'd rocked her world since the first time she laid eyes on him.

She was fourteen; he was seventeen, and it was more than his age that kept him off-limits. He was a Butler—an unmentionable name in the Avila home.

Even then, Maddox was all man. Six feet three, with steel blue eyes that danced when he smiled, Mad always looked as though he knew something scandalous that no one else did. He'd always kept his dark hair short, even when he was younger.

His rock-hard torso would rival any gym rat's, but his body was that of a man who hoisted barrels full of wine like they were ten-pound bags of potatoes.

His face was chiseled, rugged, and weathered from days spent in the vineyard heat—with a mischievous smile framed by a dark beard that hid the dimples she sometimes forgot were there. While the women in the Butler family were fair with vibrant red hair, the men wore their olive skin like a suit of armor. His trail of dark hair was perfectly placed, trailing down from his brawny neck, over his rough-hewn abs, to his pelvis.

The full-sleeve tattoos on both of his arms married traditional tribal with Celtic designs, and stopped just short of his hands. Splayed, those hands could cover her ample breasts, their power seeping into her, driving her to the edge with little but their heat, and then be equally gentle when his calloused fingers rolled her nipples.

Alex sighed, knowing those hands would not cover her body tonight. Missing them, missing the fullness she experienced only when Mad's body penetrated hers, was what kept her coming back to him, even when she knew they were destined to combust.

Maddox drove along Adelaida Trail, leaving the Wolf family's property, past Los Caballeros, the ranch her father's forefathers carved into the Paso Robles wine region, and finally, past the split-rail fence that symbolically marked the division between Los Cab and Butler Ranch.

She never took the views for granted, even though she'd lived here all her life. Deep green oak trees scattered the land kept open for livestock, while the brighter greens of the rows upon rows of vineyards cut through the golden hillsides.

"Secret's out," Maddox mumbled.

"What do you mean?"

"Uncle Maddox and Aunt Alex."

"I don't follow."

"Even your best friend had no clue about us, Al. Don't you think our families are beginning to catch on?"

Alex glanced at the boys in the back seat. As much as she hated seeing their faces glued to their smartphones, this time she appreciated the headphones that blocked out her conversation with Maddox. "Us? We're friends. That isn't a secret."

Mad rolled his eyes. "Friends who host slumber parties together."

"Don't make more of it than it is."

Usually by the time either one of them thought about divulging their "relationship," it was over anyway. They'd have a few days and nights of crazy, hot, monkey sex, and then go for weeks without being able to stand the sight of each other. It had been that way between them for years.

"What's your plan for tonight—pizza and movies? I can tell you they won't—"

"Not remotely close."

"What, then?"

"You'll see."

—:—

Maddox pulled his truck into the barn that doubled as his garage and overflow storage. His father, who should've been a titan of technology rather than a ranch and winery owner, had rigged the oversized alley doors so they opened inward when his truck got close enough. It wasn't just his truck, they would open for any vehicle that pulled up that close. Outside of his family, no one but Alex knew the trick to it.

"Ready, boys? It's adventure time." Maddox opened the back passenger door, and both boys climbed out.

"What kind of adventure?" Finn, the younger of Peyton's sons, asked.

"All kinds. I thought we'd go for a trail ride, stop in the caves."

"You're gonna take us in the caves?" Jamison's eyes opened wide. "Kade promised, but…"

"I know, Jamie." Maddox rested his hand on Jamison's shoulder.

The first wine cave on Butler Ranch was only about a thousand square feet, at the most. A few years ago, Maddox had hired an outfit out of the Burgundy region of France who specialized in subterranean caves to come and survey the site for expansion. The project took five years to complete, two years longer than the original schedule, and then it had taken them six months to organize the various barrel storage rooms and move furniture into the private areas.

"What's this about the caves?" Alex had gone inside shortly after he pulled into the garage. Now that she was back, she didn't look so good.

"Maddox is taking us on a trail ride, and then we're going in the caves." Finn rubbed his hands together, his feet shifting back and forth.

"Do you need to use the bathroom, honey?" Alex asked.

"Nah. I'm just really excited."

"You should be. I haven't even been invited into the caves yet." Alex looked over the boys' heads and mouthed, "What the hell?"

"Almost no one, outside of my brothers, the construction crew, and winery staff, has been in the caves yet."

The boys grabbed their bags, and Maddox showed them the way through the barn and out the stone path to where the cottages sat. His was the smaller of the two Scottish-style stone structures his father had built. Both were two-storied replications of the main house. His brother Naughton lived in the larger one, and since Kade died, Brodie had been living there with him.

Kade would sometimes stay in the apartment above the main barrel room when he was home on leave, but it had sat empty for over a year.

"Bedrooms are upstairs, boys. Yours are the ones with made beds. Sort out who wants to stay in which." Maddox opened the door for the boys and pointed them in the direction of the stairs, but hung back to talk to Alex.

"Everything okay, Al?"

"Why wouldn't it be?"

Instead of answering, he put his arms around her and pulled her close. Her body stiffened, but when he ran his fingers through her hair, she relaxed.

"You wanna tell me what the mystery is?"

She shook her head and put her arms around his waist.

That was progress. At least she admitted there was a mystery. Sort of.

"I know I said it was a sleepover with both of us, but the caves, Maddox? I'm not sure…I mean, are you planning on sleeping down there?"

"I was, but if you don't feel up to it, we can pretend they're man caves for tonight."

She half-laughed and turned so he couldn't see her face.

Maddox turned her back around. "You look like shit, Al."

"Thanks, Mad. Always the charmer." She tried to pull away again, but he held her tight. "You don't have to stay. I know I complained about being volunteered for this, but I can handle it on my own."

"I feel okay right now…"

"Is whatever it is contagious?" It wasn't like he was a germaphobe, but if she was sick, shouldn't she go home before he or the boys caught whatever it was?

"No, it isn't." She pulled away from him. "You're such a jerk."

"How does not wanting to catch whatever you've got make me a jerk?"

"It's not contagious, okay?" Alex stormed into the downstairs bathroom and slammed the door behind her.

"Tell you what," Maddox said to the boys when they came back downstairs. "We'll go for a ride, not too far out, stop by the caves on our way back, and you and your Aunt Alex can decide whether you want to sleep down there tonight."

Finn started to grumble, but Jamison cuffed him a good one before he could say too much.

"Don't hit him." Alex nudged Jamison when she came out of the bathroom. "That'll cost you ten."

"What? Since when? Only curse words cost money."

"Since I said so. You think swearing is worse than hitting? I don't."

Jamison groaned, and Finn laughed.

Maddox rubbed his chest, listening to the two boys bicker. They were just like him and Kade at that age. God, he missed his older brother.

"So what's the plan?"

Alex looked better than she had a few minutes ago.

"We're gonna ride, and then we're stopping to see if you want to sleep in the caves. You're gonna want to, right?" When Finn put his arms around Alex's waist, she went back to looking like shit. Maybe she ate something that didn't agree with her, although this had been going on for at least a couple of weeks.

"Give me a minute." Alex went into the kitchen, opened the fridge door, and closed it again. She walked over to the pantry and did the same thing.

"What are you looking for?" Maddox asked.

"What's it look like? Something to eat."

There was a certain surliness in Alex that Maddox had grown accustomed to. Typically it spelled the end of their friends-with-benefits time together. Any minute, he expected her to tell the boys to pack their stuff and load it into her car. Instead, she stood with her hands on her hips, staring at him.

"What?"

"I'm hungry," she huffed.

"Yeah? So?"

"What the hell, Maddox? You don't have any food in the house?"

He caught the look on Jamison's face out of the corner of his eye. The kid was just about to call Alex out on the curse word, but evidently, thought better of it. Maddox didn't blame him. Saying anything to Alex right now would be like poking a grizzly bear.

Maddox walked into the kitchen and out the back door, motioning for Alex to follow.

"What's up, Al? And don't say it's nothing. You've known me how long? Twenty years, and I have never had food in the house. Never."

"You'd think…"

"What? Finish your sentence. Wait, let me. You'd think that having two boys spending the night in my house, I would have thought to buy some food. Am I right?" Maddox held up his hand. "No, don't answer."

"Never mind."

"That's right. You didn't exactly give me any warning."

Maddox went back into the kitchen. "Hey, boys, let's go see what my ma has in her kitchen. I've been bachin' it a little too long."

"What's bachin'?" Finn asked as they walked up the stone path to his parents' house.

"Bein' a bachelor. Guys like me don't always remember to stock up on food. This time of year, I spend as much time helpin' Naughton out in the field as I do in the house."

"How's the bloom?" Alex asked absentmindedly, looking over at the nearest vineyard.

"Full."

She nodded her head.

The one thing he and Alex could always talk about were the vineyards. They spoke in the shorthand only those raised in the vines understood.

His mother was standing in the kitchen when Maddox opened the door.

"Who's this, visiting my kitchen?" she said in her thick Scottish brogue.

"Hi, Sorcha." Alex kissed her cheek.

"How are you, sweetheart?" His mother cupped Alex's cheek with her hand.

Maddox watched the exchange, wondering if his ma knew what was up with Alex.

"Hungry, and whatever that is, smells really good."

"This be my Scottish stew, lass. You boys hungry too?"

Jamison and Finn nodded their heads.

"Go wash your hands. Maddox, you too, and tell your da that we'll eat in the dining room."

—:—

"He wants to take the boys out riding and then to the caves," Alex said once Maddox ushered them out of the kitchen.

"He's aff his heid!"

Alex laughed. "I agree, he's crazy."

"Who's crazy?" Maddox came back into the kitchen.

"You *dinnae* take those wee ones to the caves." Sorcha smacked the back of his head.

"Ow!" Maddox rubbed his head, looked at Alex, and smirked.

Sorcha carried the pot of stew out of the kitchen, shaking her head, and mumbling something Alex couldn't understand.

"You're gonna love the caves, baby."

"Oh, yeah?" Alex leaned her body into his.

—:—

That was all the invitation he needed. Maddox lifted her. "Put your legs around me."

When she hooked her feet behind him, he rested her bottom on the counter, shifting her so her warmth pressed against him.

"What you do to me, girl," he growled, pulling her tighter to him. "I could take you right here, right now, in my ma's kitchen." He could feel her hardened nipples brushing against his chest through his thin shirt.

"God, Mad. Why do we always end up this way?" she groaned, but pressed her body harder against his.

"Our bodies know what our heads refuse to accept, Alex."

"But—"

Before she could protest, like he knew she would, Maddox plundered her mouth.

No one kissed him back the way Alex did, but then he was the one who'd taught her how. Alex Avila may have kissed other boys in the years he'd known her, but he was the one who'd kissed her first.

***

The first time they kissed was right before his eighteenth birthday. She and a group of friends had been following him and Naughton around all night.

"Who's that, Naught?"

"Who?"

Maddox stopped at a game booth on the midway of the county fair, and pointed at the pack of girls who had been stalking him and his brother for the past two hours.

"They look familiar, but I only know one." Naughton pointed. "That's Bianca Ramirez."

Maddox knew Bianca, but she wasn't the one who'd caught his attention. It was the other girl, who looked a lot like her.

"That one. Who is she?" When Maddox pointed right at Alex, she smiled. Instead of looking away, she met his gaze and held it.

"No idea."

Maddox nodded his head and motioned for her to come closer. "What's your name?"

"Alex." She stood in front of him, but looked down at the ground.

"I'm Maddox."

"I know who you are."

"What's your last name, Alex?"

"Avila."

"You shouldn't be talking to me if you know who I am."

"You know who I am, and you're talking to me."

The feud between the Avilas and Butlers went back to the year Laird Butler had bested Alfonso Avila with his first release of Zinfandel.

The proud Hispanic patriarch couldn't accept Laird's gold medal win at the annual wine festival, when his own Zin hadn't medaled at all. He accused Laird of paying off the judges. Maddox's father had been furious, and the two men came close to blows before several other winemakers stepped in and separated them.

From that day forward, the Avila name became unmentionable in the Butler house. It wasn't easy for the two families to avoid one another, given Butler land bordered the southernmost boundaries of Avila's Los Caballeros Ranch, but they managed.

"We're both playing with fire, Alex Avila," he said to her that night.

And they had been. The girl he spent a couple of hours kissing wasn't just an Avila; she was only fifteen years old.

Kade was home on leave from the Marines, and lit into him. "Stay the hell away from her, Maddox. She's a kid and you're a man. If Da finds out you've been spending time with an Avila, you know what'll happen."

At the time, Maddox had been more concerned with Kade's reaction than what he expected from his father. His father's anger would've been because of the girl's family. Kade was pissed at Maddox because of her age.

"She looks a lot older," Maddox tried to defend himself.

Kade made him promise not to have anything to do with her from then on. It was the first promise Maddox made to his brother, knowing full well he'd break it.

2

Peyton's boys were exhausted, so instead of going to the caves after their ride, they took the horses back to the stables and then walked over to Mad's cottage.

The day had taken an emotional toll on everyone, especially her godsons, who'd lived a roller coaster ride of a life for the past year.

First Kade, who they'd gotten so close to, was killed in Afghanistan. Then Brodie, who the boys bonded with almost immediately in spite of Peyton's efforts to keep them from doing so, disappeared from their mother's life and theirs. On top of that, their mother was pregnant and, first, had been hospitalized, and then on bed rest. While they stayed with Peyton's parents, the boys still helped their grandparents care for their mother.

When she'd received the news of Brodie's plane crash, Peyton insisted on being honest with Jamison and Finn about what had happened. They'd accepted Brodie's death in the same way they accepted Kade's.

After Maddox and Naughton found Brodie had survived the crash, and brought him back to California from Argentina, Peyton refused to see him or let him see her boys. Earlier today, Alex's intervention brought Brodie to Peyton's parents' place, where he was finally able to convince Peyton to give him another chance.

Jamie and Finn witnessed most of it—watching the events of the day play out like a movie. How could a ten- and eight-year-old not be exhausted after a day like that?

Alex was exhausted for the same reason, but there was more. She stood outside the bedroom where she'd sat with Jamie and Finn until they fell asleep, dreading the walk downstairs and the conversation she'd be forced to have with Maddox when she got there.

Maddox had his back to her and was looking out the window when she came into the living room.

"They asleep?" he asked without turning around.

"It didn't take long, and I'm not far behind."

When Maddox turned around, his hands were in his pockets. "Have a seat."

She sat in the closest chair.

"What's going on with you, Alex? Be honest with me."

"It's nothing."

"Bullshit."

"I haven't told you, because I'm not sure."

"Told me what?"

Alex leaned forward and put her head in her hands. She hated the way Maddox was talking to her, like she was a badly behaved child. Whenever he acted this way, she'd leave and wouldn't talk to him for weeks.

"Dammit, Alex! Answer me. What haven't you told me?"

"I think I'm pregnant."

—:—

"I see." Maddox turned his back to her again and looked out the window. The sky was clear, and the moon shone bright, casting light on the vines that danced in the soft breeze. He could feel her eyes on his back, knew she was waiting for him to say more.

"If I am…"

He waited, and when she didn't continue, he turned around. "If you are…what?"

"It's yours."

"I didn't doubt that, Al." He sat on the sofa and held his hand out. "Come here."

Alex sat next to him and rested her back against him.

"You said you think…"

She nodded.

"No test?"

She shook her head. "Not yet."

"If you are…"

Alex shrugged. "I have no idea."

"Baby changes a lot, Al."

She tensed and tried to move away, but Maddox put his arm around her waist and held her against him.

"It doesn't have to."

"What? Change things?"

"Not for you."

"Is that what you think?"

Alex rested her head against him. "I don't have a choice, but you do."

Maddox turned her so she faced him. "You know me better than that."

She shrugged again. "I'm not that late."

"How late?"

"Three weeks."

—:—

"Alex…" He stood and pulled her up with him.

She hated the way he said her name as much as she loved it. All the power in his rock-hard muscles came through his voice. He could whisper, and his force would still be unleashed.

She melded against him. Her curves slid into his like they were two halves of something broken being put back together.

"There's a lot we don't have a choice about, darlin'," he breathed. "Neither of us do."

He was right; they didn't. She'd never been able to resist Maddox Butler. When he lifted her into his arms and carried her up the stairs to his bedroom, her hand gripped his neck and brought his lips closer to hers. If the rest of their relationship could work as well as the sex did, they'd be soulmates, but it didn't, and after so many years, there was no reason to think it ever would.

"Clothes off, Alex," he said, resting her body on his bed. He stood in front of her, arms folded, waiting while she pulled her blouse over her head and unzipped her jeans. As she slowly exposed more skin, Maddox's eyes took in her body like it was the first time he'd seen it, yet those eyes, his hands, and the rest of him, knew her body like a back road he drove every day of his life.

"Turn over," he demanded once she was naked.

She rolled to her stomach and waited for his touch. Shivers ran down her spine as his fingers worked their way up the back of her legs. He kneaded the flesh of her behind with hands that were big enough to circle her waist, while his lips kissed up her spine. He'd taken off his shirt, so the hair on his chest tickled her back when he rested his body on top of hers.

"You know where to put your hands, Alex." He stilled, waiting for her to grasp the metal frame of the headboard.

With her arms stretched out, Maddox worked his lips along the side of her body, from her hip to her waist. When he reached her breast, he rolled her under him, just slightly, to give his mouth access.

She flinched when his teeth grazed her nipple, shocked by their tenderness. He bit and released her, licking the sting away. He'd removed his belt and unfastened the button at the top of his jeans. His zipper, lowered just slightly, scratched against the back of her thighs.

Alex knew better than to tell Maddox to hurry. He never had, and he never would, this he told her time and time again. He'd draw out his body's assault on hers until she reached the point where every nerve ending was frayed, and her desire for him reached a frenzy.

—:—

Jeans off, Maddox lined his bareness up against her. If Alex was already pregnant, there was no reason for them to use a condom.

It had been his resolute desire to finally feel her this way that got her in this situation. It had been a risk to take her without a condom, even though she was on birth control. Accidents happened. Drugs failed. Babies were conceived. He wasn't a kid; he understood the possible consequences.

They both knew the day would come when they'd be forced to grow up, quit jerking each other around, and just figure it out. Looked like that day had arrived.

He waited while her body adjusted to his, and then moved slowly in and out, thrusting deeper each time. Alex's soft mewls grew louder. He could take her over the edge, but he wanted to see her face when she fell. He separated himself from her and flipped her onto her back.

"Come on, baby. Give it to me," he rasped just before Alex squeezed her eyes closed and let her head fall from side to side. "That's my girl," he coaxed.

Maddox let the legs he'd been holding fall to the bed and grasped her hips. "Once more," he groaned.

Before she could roll away, Maddox covered her mouth with his, pressing down hard, devouring her with his lips.

No other woman could make him feel the unabandoned passion that Alex brought out in him. He couldn't stay away from her. He was addicted to the way she made him feel.

Alex turned her back to his front and drew the blanket up over her shoulders. Maddox slid his body behind her and put his arm around her waist.

"Move in with me, Alex."

—:—

She didn't answer. There was no reason to. She moved his arm from around her waist and got out of bed. "Bathroom," she muttered, but that wasn't why she got up.

She closed the door between the bedroom and en-suite bath, and sat on the edge of the two-person jetted tub. What she'd give to fill it, climb in, and let the warm water soak away her worries. Instead, she hoped Maddox would soon fall asleep, and she'd be left alone to think.

Ten minutes later, she turned the door knob, hoping she could sneak in without waking him, but he wasn't asleep; he was sitting up in bed, waiting for her.

"Maddox, please…"

"I told you earlier; your secret's out."

"You didn't want anyone to know about us any more than I did."

"I'm not ashamed of our relationship, Al."

"I'm not ashamed either, but I don't think you can call what we've been doing a relationship."

"What would you call it, then? Fucking?"

"You don't have to be crass."

"Then answer me. What would you call it?"

She leaned down to pick up her clothes, but he caught her arm in his hand.

"Get back in bed."

"Don't tell me what to do, Mad."

"You liked it an hour ago. In fact you've always liked it."

"You're such an asshole."

"Am I? The way I remember it, you were willing to do whatever I told you to do."

"This is why I hate you, Maddox."

He pulled her on top of him. "Yeah? You hate me? I can feel how much you hate me, Alex."

Maddox wrapped her hair in his hand and pulled her down so her lips touched his. When he kissed her, she melted. He was right, this wasn't why she hated him; this was why she hated herself.

Soft lips kissing her shoulder lured her out of a deep sleep. "I'm sorry," Maddox whispered in her ear.

She opened her eyes and stared into his deep blue ones. "I'm sorry, too."

"I'm glad you stayed."

"This time." She laughed, admitting silently that their arguments were often short-lived, given her typical reaction was to walk away.

Maddox moved the blankets away from her body, scattered kisses over her belly, and then rested his head just below her abdomen. "I want this baby, Alex."

She rested her hand on his head, wishing he hadn't forced her to tell him. "I'll check on the boys if you make coffee."

"Yeah, that's what I figured." He shook his head.

"I'm not interested in discussing your misguided sense of obligation when I'm not even sure there is a baby." Alex got out of bed, grabbed her clothes, and got dressed.

Maddox stood near the bedroom door, watching.

"Go away," she scowled, surprised when he turned around and left the room.

—:—

The boys were awake; Maddox could hear them talking. He looked in one of the bedrooms, and the bed was still made. He knocked on the door of the other room, remembering Alex had told him they'd probably feel more comfortable sleeping in the same room.

"Hey, guys," he said when they told him to come in. "Breakfast requests?"

Finn looked at Jamison, who shrugged his shoulders. "We're good with whatever."

"Either one of you happen to know what Alex's favorite thing is to have for breakfast?"

"Junk food," they answered in unison.

"Right," Maddox laughed. "Cold pizza. I was thinking something more along the lines of waffles."

"Waffles are good," Finn murmured.

"But not as good as cold pizza?"

"Finn," Jamison admonished. "Waffles would be great, thanks."

"Waffles?" Alex stood behind Maddox, peeking over his shoulder. "Who's making waffles?"

"I am."

"You sneak out to the grocery store last night?"

"Didn't have to. Ma dropped off breakfast fixins' this morning."

"You're so spoiled."

Maddox wanted to be mad at her, but when he turned around and she smiled at him, he couldn't. Instead, he swatted her bottom as he walked past her. "Come help me, woman."

—:—

"So bossy." She winked at Jamison and Finn. "There might be some pizza hidden in the back of Mad's fridge if you're brave enough to risk it."

The boys climbed out of bed and ran past Alex on their way downstairs.

"Save me a piece," she hollered after them.

They reminded her of how her two youngest brothers were when they were kids. Now they both towered over her, not that she saw either of them very often.

Three of her brothers still lived in Paso Robles. Gabe, the oldest, was the principal winemaker. Enzo, less than two years older than Alex, oversaw compliance with licensing and labor, as well as being the secondary label winemaker. Trevino, also known as Trev, two years younger than her, was responsible for wine sales and ran the tasting room.

Something was up with Enzo. Every time she saw him lately, he seemed troubled. She tried to talk to Gabe about it, but he dismissed it, and her, as nothing but an annoyance. Maybe that's what Enzo's problem was. He was tired of Gabe dismissing him.

Cristobal, second oldest to Gabe, was the chief medical officer for Geneco, a Palo Alto-based research-based corporation whose mission was to understand and influence the genetic basis of aging.

Her baby brothers, Salazar and Rascon, were PRCA team-ropers, on the road eleven months of the year. Like Jamison and Finn, they were two years apart. Salazar, whom everyone called Snapper, was the header. Their youngest brother, Rascon, whom everyone called Kick, was the heeler.

If their father were still alive, he never would've allowed the boys to become professional rodeo cowboys, but according to the national earnings reports, both her brothers netted over a quarter of a million dollars in winnings, plus the money they made from sponsorships and endorsements. The wine business could be lucrative, but Alex doubted Snapper and Kick would've been pulling in that kind of cash if they still worked for Gabe at Los Caballeros Winery.

"Where's Alex?" she heard Maddox bellow from downstairs, knowing it was meant for her to hear more than Jamie and Finn.

"Coming," she answered, but not loud enough for him to hear.

—:—

It was the bacon Maddox threw on the griddle that he knew would entice Alex to the kitchen. Bacon had always been her weakness. He swore she could eat it every meal, every day. When she walked in, he handed her a plate. "Crispy today?" No one else he knew ordered bacon cooked a particular way based on her mood.

"No, thanks. Limp is good." She winked.

God, what she did to him. If two little boys weren't watching, he'd make her his breakfast. He'd never been able to get enough of her, not since the very first time.

***

Maddox ran into Alex everywhere he went the summer after she graduated from high school. If she was with her mother and father, or if he was with his parents, they'd ignore each other, the way their parents did.

If he was with Kade or Brodie, he'd ignore her too, which he knew hurt her feelings. But if he was with Naughton or alone, he'd talk to her. He'd kept his distance since they met, three years prior, but now that she was over eighteen, there was no reason for him to keep doing so.

Temperatures in the summer months in Paso Robles averaged in the nineties, with many days over one hundred degrees. Maddox was at Lake Naco, water skiing with friends, when he saw Alex sitting on the beach. She was with her cousin and was wearing the sexiest red bikini he'd ever seen.

Just as the boat Maddox was on pulled up to the dock, Alex walked into the shallow water near the shore. He watched her wade in, and when the water reached her waist, Maddox dove from the boat. She watched him go underwater, and didn't act surprised when he grabbed her around the waist, slid his body up hers, and surfaced, their lips close to touching when he did.

She wrapped her arms around his neck, and her legs around his waist. Maddox grasped her bottom and held her close to him. "You feel me, Alex?"

"I feel you, Maddox. You gonna tease me like you did three years ago?"

Maddox laughed but narrowed his gaze, staring into her brown, almost-black eyes. "You, little girl, were the one teasing me."

"I haven't been a little girl for a long time, Maddox Butler. In fact, I wasn't a little girl the night you met me, and I can assure you, I'm not a little girl right now."

"No, you're not." With her arms still clasped around his neck, Maddox leaned forward and kissed her. It had been three years since he kissed her the night of the county fair, but her lips felt the same as he remembered.

"You sure about this?" he asked. "You could get yourself in a lot of trouble."

"Have you forgotten that I have six brothers, all of whom hate your family as much as my father does?"

"What are you saying, that I could be the one in trouble?"

She smiled and nodded.

"You're worth it." Maddox kissed her again, and then released her and swam away.

They saw each other every chance they had that summer. Sometimes they'd meet at the lake; sometimes they'd both ride out over the hills of their adjoining property, tether their horses, and spend hours under a sprawling oak tree.

He got to know the curves of Alex's body that summer, but it wasn't until they were both due to leave for college that lips and hands were no longer enough.

Maddox held back more than Alex, but the idea of leaving for college not knowing how it felt to be buried inside her, left him unable to resist any longer.

"I want you, Alex," Maddox said one day as they lay on a blanket under the oak tree. He'd started bringing one along a few weeks ago, around the same time Alex started bringing a picnic for them to share. "I don't want to wait."

Alex didn't answer him with words, but when she slid her shorts and panties down her long legs and threw them to the side of the blanket, he knew she didn't want to wait either.

***

He took her virginity that day, and in hindsight, Alex took away any chance that another woman could ever satisfy him again.

—:—

"You're deep in thought." Alex regretted the words as soon as she spoke them.

"Thinking about us, Alex. That summer, before you left for San Diego and I went back to Davis."

She felt the heat flood her cheeks, remembering how crazy she was about him then, and how relentlessly she'd pursued him. She'd made up her mind that she was going to lose her virginity to Maddox before the end of the summer, and became obsessed with making it happen.

He reached around and drew her into him. "I want you just as much now as I did then. Maybe more."

Alex tried to back away, but he held her close. She glanced over at Jamison and Finn, who were both absorbed in the latest "Fast and Furious" movie Mad must've downloaded for them.

"Knock, knock, anybody home?" Brodie walked in the front door and stopped to talk to Jamie and Finn.

Before she could wriggle away from him, Maddox planted a kiss on her that made her toes curl.

"Why do you fight me, Alex?"

"I don't know." It was hard for her to admit, and as she said the words, her eyes filled with tears. When he was like this, she wondered why she ever got mad at him, but then there were other times when she wondered why she thought she liked him.

"Don't keep fighting it. Let go, Alex."

"I can't." Alex pulled away from him and went into the other room to talk to Brodie.

"How are things between you and Peyton?" Alex asked Brodie, who looked at his phone before answering.

"She's reading a letter from Kade."

"Oh?"

"We opened the box together. There was a letter at the bottom."

Alex followed Brodie into the kitchen where Mad was washing dishes from breakfast.

"I can do that," she offered.

"How about you help?"

She picked up a towel and dried the dishes he set in a rack on the counter.

"She's reading it now?" Maddox asked.

"Yeah. I wasn't sure if you heard me. I didn't want the boys to know, although I don't know why not."

"She'll tell them when she's ready. She doesn't keep stuff from them, Brodie." Alex hoped one day she'd be half the mother Peyton was, although she wasn't sure she was ready for it yet.

When his phone buzzed, Brodie hurried out the front door without saying another word to her, Maddox, or the boys.

"That was weird." Alex looked out the front window and saw Brodie walk in the back door of the house he and Naughton shared.

"Think he'll move in with her?" Alex asked Maddox.

"Don't you?"

"Her place is pretty small. Just three bedrooms, which I guess would be okay. Although, I'm sure they'll look for a bigger place eventually."

If she was pregnant, and Maddox talked her into moving in with him, they wouldn't live in a house on his parents' ranch for the rest of their lives, would they?

It would be hard for Alex to give up the first house she bought on her own. She loved her little place near the beach, although she understood that Maddox would never feel comfortable in it.

Other than when he was at college, Mad had never lived anywhere other than on this ranch. A little house in a neighborhood where you could practically reach your arm out the window and touch the house next door made him feel claustrophobic. She almost always stayed here with him. Sometimes it bothered her, mainly when she was irritated with him about something else. "Why do I always have to come to you?" she'd ask him.

"I'll come and get you," he'd offer.

"Why can't you stay at my house?"

"You gonna be able to keep quiet, Alex? What will your neighbors say when we keep 'em awake all night?"

It was a lousy argument, but one she usually gave into anyway. She could count on one hand the number of times he'd stayed with her.

The front door flew open, and Peyton came inside, followed closely by Brodie. When Jamison and Finn saw her, they both jumped up and ran to hug her. Alex watched Peyton squeeze them tight, and then kneel down on the floor. Alex joined them as Peyton lifted her left hand and pointed to the ring.

"Brodie asked me to marry him," she said to the boys. "What do you think?"

Alex couldn't hear whether they answered or not amidst the shouting and cheers. Naughton came in the front door a few minutes later, followed by Laird and Sorcha.

With all the commotion, it was easy for her to slip out the back door of Mad's house and climb in her car unnoticed. She was far enough away that he couldn't stop her by the time she saw him come out the back door.

3

She didn't feel like going home yet. Maybe she'd stop at Los Cab, see her mom, and talk one of her brothers into going for a ride with her.

She'd purchased her four-year-old gelding, Malachi, a year ago. He'd been ranch-bred and had the sweetest nature. He willingly went along through the hills, creek beds, and even alongside the vineyards.

"Ah, mi amor, mija." Her mother stood and hugged her when she opened the front door.

"Hi, Mama."

"Come and sit. What's on your mind, Alex?"

"Brodie just asked Peyton to marry him."

Her mother clapped her hands together and looked up at the ceiling. "Praise the Holy Father," she whispered.

"You sound like Sorcha," Alex laughed. "I think she said the very same thing."

"It's a blessing, *mija.* Don't you agree?"

"Of course I do. I couldn't be happier for Peyton. She's so much better off with Brodie than she would've been with Kade, not that I wanted anything bad to happen to him."

Her mother's eyes grew dark, and she looked away for a moment. When she turned back around, she was smiling again.

"What was that?"

Instead of answering, her mother patted Alex's hand and stood. "What can I get you to eat? Have you had lunch?"

She'd had breakfast, but she was hungry again. "Not yet."

"Join me, then." Her mother motioned for Alex to follow her into the kitchen.

Alex sat at the table and watched her mother pull things out of the refrigerator. She didn't know what she was making, but whatever it was would be good.

The back door flew open, and Gabe came inside, followed by Enzo and Trev.

"Hey, Al, what's shakin'?" Trev leaned down to kiss her cheek.

"*¡Por Dios!*" Her mother put her hand on her heart. "You startled me."

One by one, Alex's brothers kissed their mother's cheek and then went to the sink to wash their hands.

"What's for lunch?" Gabe asked.

She waved her hands over the food. "This."

"As if that's an answer, Mama." Enzo smiled. "What are you doin' here, Alex? Everything okay?"

"She doesn't need a reason to come and see her *madre*."

"Ow!" Enzo jumped when their mother swatted him with a wooden spoon.

"I was on my way back to Cambria and decided to stop in and go for a ride. Any of you interested in going with me."

"I will," Enzo spoke up. His expression changed when Gabe glared at him.

"Don't let him intimidate you, *mijo,*" their mother warned.

"Maybe a short one."

Alex looked at her phone. It was almost two, and while Sam and Addy, their regular tasting room employees, would have everything covered, especially given this was the first weekday they'd been open in weeks, she still felt as though she should go in and see if they needed help.

"I'll see how Sam and Addy are doing," she said more to herself than to her mother or brothers.

Her phone buzzed, and she considered not looking at it. Whatever Maddox had to say wouldn't be good. Instead, the text was from Peyton.

Where did you go?

Stopped at Los Cab. Riding before I go to Stave.

Alex and Peyton had been running the tasting room they'd jointly named Stave, since shortly after they graduated from college. What had once been an adjunct tasting room for Wolf Family Vintners, had grown into a very successful outlet for all of the wineries in the Westside Winery Collaborative. In addition to co-managing Stave, Alex also served as the organization's marketing director.

You didn't say anything. You just left.

Had to get away from Maddox, she wrote, as though that would explain everything. *Sorry,* she added.

I have stuff to tell you.

Before Peyton got involved with Brodie, Alex spent almost every evening with her and the boys. Her first instinct was to tell Peyton she'd come over later, but it wasn't that easy anymore.

How are you feeling? She asked instead.

That's the news. Released from bed rest.

Seriously?

Yep. Brodie promised to bring me by Stave later.

You sure? Alex hoped so. She had stuff to tell Peyton, too.

She helped her mother clean up from lunch, and went out to the barn. She missed her horse, the one big disadvantage of living in Cambria. There was nowhere for her to keep Malachi in town.

The contrast between Malachi's thick, black mane and gray coat was one of the reasons she'd bid on him at the auction, and kept bidding until he was hers.

It looked as though the guys who worked in the barns hadn't groomed her horse yet, but Alex didn't mind. She loved to groom Malachi herself, even though she wasn't out here as much as she should be.

There was a certain peace that came with caring for her horse. While her brothers complained about having to work in the stables, Alex never minded it. She'd much rather be here than out in the vines.

"Hey, my sweet boy." Alex ran her hand over his withers.

Malachi turned his head and nudged her, and Alex stroked his face.

"Let's ride, buddy."

She was partway down her favorite trail when she felt lightheaded. "Better head back, sweet boy."

Her stomach hurt, most likely because she wasn't used to eating as much as she had between breakfast and the feast her mom had put together for lunch.

"Short ride, I know, but I'm not feeling so good," Alex said to her horse.

She got him settled, went inside to say goodbye to her mother, and got on the road.

When she drove past the gates of Butler Ranch, her stomach hurt worse, and by the time she got to Cambria, she wasn't sure it was a good idea to go to Stave. Instead, she went home. If she was coming down with the flu, she shouldn't be around customers.

Alex made it to her driveway, not sure if she had the strength to get out of the car.

Where are you? She texted Peyton.

Home. Be in soon.

Came home. Feeling sick.

Need anything?

Don't want you to get sick.

She felt lightheaded and let her eyes drift closed.

"Is she okay?" Alex heard Peyton asked.

She opened her eyes, and Brodie was leaning down, his hand on her forehead.

"You're burning up, Alex. Let's get you in the house."

Brodie reached in and lifted her out of the car.

"Brodie!" Peyton gasped.

"What?"

Alex saw Peyton shake her head and motion at Brodie's truck.

Alex would ask them what was wrong, but she didn't have the strength. Instead, she rested her head against Brodie and let her eyes drift closed again.

Her mom was running her fingers through Alex's hair when she woke up.

"Where am I?"

"At the hospital, *mija,*" her mom whispered.

Alex closed her eyes again. Between Peyton, Brodie, and Sorcha, she'd spent too much time at this place in the past few weeks. The last thing she remembered was Brodie carrying her to his truck. After that, nothing.

"Why am I here?" she asked without opening her eyes.

"Peyton and Brodie found you in the car in your driveway, passed out, *mija.*"

"Where's Maddox?" Alex turned her head to the side, not wanting to see the recrimination in her mother's eyes.

"In the hall. Do you want to see him?"

"Can you tell him I'll call him later?"

Her mother shook her head.

"I don't want to see him right now, Mama."

Her mother shook her head again, but stood and walked out of the room. Alex closed her eyes and waited. There was a fifty-fifty chance that Maddox would be the one walking back in instead of her mother.

Alex breathed a sigh of relief when the door opened and her mother came back in.

"He left."

—:—

Maddox got in the elevator. He'd go downstairs, but he wouldn't leave. He knew Alex well enough to know she'd want to be alone, but not for long. In fact, he predicted that within the hour, she'd call and ask him to come back. In the meantime, he'd stay close by.

"Can I see her?" Peyton asked when he came in the waiting room.

"You can try."

Peyton nodded her head and walked in the direction of the elevator. He didn't need to explain what he meant. She knew Alex well enough to know she'd refuse to see him, but Peyton would be allowed in.

"Has the doctor told you anything?"

He shook his head and walked to the window. "Lucia said they're going to keep her here overnight."

"What's wrong with her, Mad?"

"I have no idea."

That wasn't true, but since Alex only told him she thought she might be pregnant, it wasn't his place to tell anyone else.

Maddox kept his back to Brodie, not wanting to see the look on his brother's face.

"You know more than you're saying."

Maddox shrugged.

Alex was the only girl among six brothers, and she had been doted on her whole life. She could do and say whatever she pleased, and she did, because she was protected by a pack of hot-tempered Hispanic men who were a lot like their father.

At least in recent years, Maddox was certain their relationship hadn't been the secret he and Alex pretended it was. The valley was small and close-knit—news of her hanging out with him would've spread quickly. The only person who should have known about it, but didn't, was Peyton.

When Alex's father died, a little over five years ago, she turned to him after not speaking to him, outside of saying hello, for over two years. It was the longest they'd gone without talking since she'd turned eighteen. Her father's death, and how hard it was on her, was the first glimpse Maddox got of the insecurity Alex hid beneath her shroud of strength.

He'd been the one to go to his father and ask that they help the Avilas when Alfonso died. Alex's father was in the vineyard when a massive heart attack took his life. He was airlifted to the same hospital Alex was in now, although Maddox heard he died before they reached the landing pad.

Her oldest brother, Gabe, had been taking over more and more of the winemaking duties at Los Caballeros, but in their grief, Maddox doubted they'd be able to get through crush without help from area winemakers and vineyard owners.

Laird Butler and his sons hadn't been the only people in the valley to help, they'd just been the ones who helped the most. With their land bordering one another's, it only made sense that they could be there more often and more easily. No one would've thought much of it if it hadn't been for the longstanding feud between the two families.

***

Laird guided Gabe through the harvest and crush that year, walking the vineyards with him. Maddox often heard his father quip, "The grapes will get better and better, until the day they start to get worse."

The first and most important decision Gabe had to make was when to pull the early varietals off the vines. When to pick each type of grape was the first irrevocable decision in the sequence of winemaking, and a time fraught with pressure, anticipation, hope, anxiety, and ultimately, joy.

As with any other form of gambling, winemakers were forced to determine when to stop the deal and live with the hand they were given. If they picked too early, the grapes wouldn't be ripe enough. If they picked too late, the grapes would be over-ripe.

There were analytical tools winemakers used to measure sugar, acid, and pH in the ripening grapes, but as much as formulas and target numbers helped zero in on when to pick, the most crucial decisions were made based on a combination of intuition and experience. Together, Laird and Gabe watched vine condition and weather, focusing on the taste and condition of the fruit.

The day they decided to pick the first grapes to ripen, that year or any other, began the busiest and most hectic time of the year for winemakers. Managing one harvest required twelve- to sixteen-hour days. With two, they worked almost around the clock. The Butlers helped the Avilas, and then the Avilas turned around and helped the Butlers.

Maddox and Naughton worked with Alex's three younger brothers, Trevino, Salazar, and Rascon, to wash and check equipment, prep barrels, and make sure the right yeasts had been ordered and were on site. They were behind schedule, but if worse came to worst, the plan was to transport the grapes and crush at Butler Ranch.

Alex had been out in the vineyards and in the winery alongside him, her brothers, and his for days that grew longer once each batch of freshly harvested grapes arrived at the winery.

Sorting the bad fruit from the good was the first step after picking, and one of the most tedious in the process, but she hadn't complained.

That year, Sauvignon Blanc was the first varietal to hit the crusher-destemmer machines. When the avalanche of grapes was processed, chaos reigned. Emotions ran high as the long days and nights wore everyone out. Laird insisted they stick to a strict schedule of breaks so each of them had a chance to sleep more than a couple of hours straight.

Gabe confided in Maddox that his own father never would've allowed it. "I can't leave. This is my duty to my family, to my father," he told Maddox.

Neither realized Laird was listening until he approached. "The more tired you are, the more mistakes you make. Go get some rest. You've earned the break. No one would agree more than your father."

Gabe finally relented and went home to sleep. When he came back several hours later, he thanked Laird and extended his hand to shake. Instead, Maddox watched his father pull Gabe into a hug.

Word spread quickly through the westside wine community that day—there was a truce between the Butlers and Avilas.

The most grueling and physically taxing part of winemaking came when the red varietals were picked.

For the white varietals, the fruit was pressed, separating it from the skins, and then the juice was put straight into tanks for fermentation. It was a relatively simple process, compared to the reds.

For wines like Cabernet Sauvignon, and other red varietals, the must, which was the combination of split skins and flesh, or pulp, went into vats, where it was left to sit.

When yeast was added to the must, converting the sugars in the grapes to alcohol and carbon dioxide, the gas would push the skins to the surface, creating what was called a cap. To extract the most color and flavor, at least twice a day, the cap formed by the skins had to be punched back down.

Everyone hated the job, yet Maddox often volunteered when others complained.

"How do you do it?" Alex asked one night when he offered to drive her home.

He laughed. "Which part?"

"How do you stay so positive?"

"I don't know. I guess I try to remind myself why I want to be a winemaker. When I spent a year working in French vineyards and wineries, that's when I really fell in love with the process."

He told her about the culture of the harvest in France, and how it was entrenched in celebration. "There were hour-and-a-half lunches every day, and at the end of harvest, there'd be grape fights in the vineyard."

When the last load of the last varietal to be harvested was delivered, clusters of grapes were scattered all over the tractor, and a guy with an accordion would play "La Vie en Rose."

"It sounds like a fairytale, but it was very real. I want it to be that way in my winery someday."

"I like that," Maddox remembered her saying. "Some people are cup-half-empty people. You've always been a cup-half-full person."

"You never know when the grapes you pick, sort, and process might turn into a great vintage. That's what it's all about, right?"

"The start of something magical."

Maddox wondered, that night, if Alex was talking about the wine or about them.

***

Since that first harvest after her father died, he and Alex had been together more than not.

She was usually the one who walked away, refused to talk to him or try to work out their differences, but Maddox had never pushed very hard. He let her come back in her own time, always believing she would.

—:—

"I told you, there's nothing to forgive," Alex told Peyton.

"I was so wrapped up in what was going on with Brodie and me, and then Lang petitioning for custody of Jamison and Finn. I knew something was up with you. I should've taken the time to talk to you."

"There was nothing to talk about." Twenty minutes ago, the doctor had come in and told her she had a mass on her ovary so large that it had blocked her menstrual cycle, and she had developed an infection.

Their plan was to surgically remove the mass and keep her ovary intact so she'd be able to get pregnant in the future. Given the infection, the surgery had to be performed almost immediately, before sepsis set in.

"Alex?"

"What, Peyton?"

"Are you pregnant?"

Alex's eyes filled with tears. "No."

"Does Maddox know what's going on?"

Alex shook her head.

"Why are you shutting him out?"

"I'm not. I just don't want to see him right now. You, of all people, should understand."

"You forced me to see Brodie."

"I didn't force you to do anything."

"Let him in, Alex. He's worried about you."

Alex's eyes widened. "You can't be serious. You're such a hypocrite. *Yesterday* you didn't want anything to do with Brodie. Now that you're engaged and everything is happily ever after with you two, you've forgotten the last few weeks?"

"I was wrong. And what you're doing now is wrong."

"Easy for you to say."

"Isn't that what you wanted for me? You wanted me to forgive Brodie. I know you did, because you told him what to say."

"I didn't tell him anything."

"You did. He told me you did."

"All I told him was not to say he was sorry until he told you the whole story about what happened that night. That's it, Peyton. And as far as my not wanting to see Maddox right now, it isn't any of your business. We aren't together in the same way you and Brodie are. We never have been."

"You're the hypocrite, Alex."

"That's enough. Let her be." Both Alex and Peyton jumped when the door opened and Maddox walked in. "Peyton, do you mind giving us a few minutes?"

Peyton stood and kissed Alex's forehead. "I love you, and that's all that really matters, Alex."

"I love you, too," Alex whispered, knowing she was going to cry, and wishing there was some way she could stop herself.

When the door closed behind Peyton, Maddox sat on the bed next to her.

"How are you feeling?"

"Fine."

"What did the doctor say?"

"I have a mass."

"You're not pregnant?"

She shook her head, and when he reached for her, buried her face in his shoulder and let herself cry.

4

"I'll be back tomorrow, and don't worry about new release night. We can skip it," Alex told Peyton.

"I can handle new release night on my own, Alex. The first trimester was the hardest." Peyton rubbed her hands over her belly. "The boys were harder for me than this little peanut."

Alex came in this morning, but after a couple of hours, Peyton suggested she go home, and Alex didn't argue. She'd been home from the hospital for over a week but still didn't feel like she had any energy.

"Are you in a lot of pain?" Peyton asked.

She was, but it had nothing to do with her surgery. How could she explain the way she felt when Peyton talked about her baby, when she didn't understand it herself? It wasn't as though she had been pregnant; the mass they removed from her body had nothing to do with a baby.

"I'm sorry, Alex."

"What for?"

Peyton rested her hands on her ever-growing tummy. Alex doubted she even knew she did it.

"That you weren't pregnant."

"No reason for you or anyone else to be sorry."

"You know what I mean."

Alex nodded. She did know.

"Go home and rest," Peyton told her.

She went home, but she didn't rest. She didn't have the energy to do anything, but she couldn't sleep either. She picked up her phone to call Maddox more times than she could count, but each time she set it back down.

What would she say? Now that they knew she wasn't pregnant, maybe it was time they parted ways for good. Maybe it had been a sign. He'd always be important to her, and she hoped they'd stay friends, but otherwise, she couldn't see anything more between them. They'd run their course.

—:—

"Son, a word when you have a minute?"

"Yeah, Da. I have a minute now."

"Come up to the house with me."

Maddox followed his father up the stone pathway that connected the winery buildings to the main house.

It was the house Maddox and his siblings grew up in. When he was a teenager, it had seemed so small. Now that his parents lived in it alone, it seemed so much bigger.

It looked like a historic Scottish farmhouse, complete with a granite facade under a slate roof. The porch that wrapped around the u-shaped structure was something his father had added after inheriting the property from his parents. He'd also added the archway they were walking through that led to a courtyard. His father stopped by the pond that sat near the middle of the yard.

"Your sisters used to sneak food out to the koi after dinner. They fed them everything—bits of meat, potatoes. Your ma and I discovered what they'd been doing when Skye tried to feed them ice cream, and Ainsley had a fit when it melted before the fish could get to it."

Maddox remembered that night. Kade had been home on leave. It was one of the rare occasions all his siblings were home for dinner together.

"How's Alex?"

"She's okay." He guessed. He didn't know for sure. He only told his father what she told him. "I'm okay," was about all she'd say before coming up with an excuse to end the call, and that was only when she actually answered.

"There's something I'd like to discuss with you."

"Go ahead, Da."

"I need to get something from the house. I'll just be a minute."

Maddox sat on the bench near the pond and watched the koi fight to get to the spot closest to him. He had nothing to feed them, so the fight was fruitless. His father came out the kitchen door, carrying a large envelope. He motioned for Maddox to join him at one of the tables on the porch.

"What's this?" Maddox asked, looking over the papers his father spread out before him.

"I got a call from Peter Wendt yesterday, asking your mother and me to come to his office."

Maddox nodded, he recognized the name. Peter was an attorney in town. Thirty years ago, Peter's father had started what was now one of the biggest law firms in the county.

His father laid out a map and pointed to an area outlined in red.

"What is this?"

"It's a two-hundred-acre parcel, west of Adelaida."

Maddox studied the map and read through some of the other materials. The property was twenty miles due west from where they sat, with views of both the coast and the wine country. There was a stocked, spring-fed pond, a seasonal creek, and an existing well with a water storage tank. The map indicated several structures on the property that had power, although it gave no indication whether they were inhabitable.

"I can't figure out where this is."

"Old Creek Road." His father smiled. They both knew of the prime vineyard location.

"Is it for sale?"

"No, Maddox. It's not for sale."

"Why are you showing me this?"

His father handed him an envelope bearing his name.

"What's this?"

His father stood and patted his shoulder. "I'll be inside."

Maddox's eyes followed his father's back as he opened the kitchen door and went into the house. He opened the envelope and pulled out a letter.

Dear Maddox,

I told you once that I couldn't imagine myself getting old. When you asked if I thought that meant something, I told you I didn't know. It was a lie. I knew it meant I wouldn't see you fulfill your dreams.

This land is yours, Maddox. What you see is not all that is there. There's much for you to discover, and I promise it is beyond your most vivid dreams.

I know you think you can't leave Butler Ranch, but you can. In fact, it's long overdue.

I love you, my brother.
Kade

Maddox let the contents of the letter sink in and covered his face with his hands.

He remembered the day they had the conversation Kade mentioned in the letter. He knew the day would come when Kade didn't return from one of his missions. It was a premonition he felt deep in his soul. Each time Kade left, Maddox told him how much he loved him, as though it was the last chance he'd have to say the words.

He wiped the tears that leaked from his eyes and studied the map again. Now that he knew approximately where the property was, the lines indicating unmarked roads made more sense.

"Son?"

He hadn't heard his father come back out to the porch.

"There was a letter from Kade in the envelope. It says the property is mine," Maddox told him.

Yes." His father picked up the pipe that sat on the porch railing, pulled his tobacco pouch out of his pocket, and methodically filled it. Once he lit the pipe, he sat back down at the table.

"When did Kade buy it?"

"I have no idea."

"It would be a lot to take on, Da."

He nodded.

"We'd have to hire someone to handle the day-to-day operation here. Did you know about this?"

Laird tapped the pipe and rested it on the railing, and shook his head.

"I need to talk to Naughton."

"A good place to start."

"I need to find him."

"Shouldn't be difficult."

Maddox pulled his phone out of his back pocket and called his brother. "Where are you?"

"South Cab Franc."

"Meet me in the stables?" Maddox could almost always talk Naught into a ride, particularly at this time of the year when things were slow in the vineyards.

His father went inside, and Maddox walked back over to the koi pond. He sat, leaned forward, and put his head in his hands.

Why had Kade written that his moving on from Butler Ranch was long overdue? Sure, in the back of his mind he dreamed of starting his own winery, one where he could make wine different from the ones his family was known for.

If this land had sat dormant, the way Maddox believed it had, the earth would be rich from its years of rest, and the vineyards could be replanted any way he saw fit.

At the ranch, he and his brothers were a team. Naughton managed the vineyards, and Maddox made the wine. Brodie was responsible for selling what he and Naught produced. Brodie could easily sell wine from both properties, but Naughton would not be able to manage both vineyards, especially given the distance between the two. Maddox could do the same, and make wine at both locations, but he'd need help too.

Maddox could hire a field manager, whom Naught could oversee, for the new property, in the same way Maddox would suggest Butler Ranch hire a winery manager.

He and his brother were equally pragmatic, but would Naught see Maddox's ideas the same way? Or would he feel abandoned? He sat with his head in his hands, wishing, as he did so often, that he could talk to Kade about this.

Naught and Kade were a lot alike. They both kept to themselves, most times preferring to be alone than with a group of people. Their sister Skye was that way too.

She was a homebody, happiest when she could care for her family and spend time with her husband and their daughter.

Skye was the only one of his siblings who cared about the barn cats, or begged their father to take in stray dogs, even orphaned calves and goats. Soon Skye would have another tiny being under her care, when her son was born.

Naughton nurtured three things—horses, vines, and the grapes that grew on them. His brother could coax the most stubborn old vines back into steady production, and coax the grapes in their vineyards to produce the most complex juice in the valley.

If Naughton wasn't in the vineyard, he was in the barns or out riding.

Most of the horses in the Butler Ranch stables were Quarter Horses or Paints. Brodie had a Morgan, and while Naughton cared for all of their horses, his personal favorite was a nine-year-old American Cream Gelding named Huck. The draft horse was huge, over seventeen hands, with four white socks and a white blaze on his face. The horse was kind and quiet—a lot like Naughton.

And Kade? He had been nurturing too. He'd taken care of his younger brothers and sisters, in a way no one realized until he died. Maddox couldn't help but wonder what else Kade had done, sensing he'd leave them all too soon.

The land was so much more than property. It was a dream Maddox never thought he could fulfill.

On your way? Naughton's text showed up on his phone.

Yeah. Be there in five.

—:—

Alex answered the knock at the door, relieved that it was her brother Cristobal and not Maddox.

"Hey, Cris." She opened the door to let him in.

"Hey, Al."

"What brings you down my way?"

"Taking a long weekend and thought I'd come see my favorite sister."

"Your only sister. How'd you know I'd be home?"

Cris raised his eyebrows and laughed. There wasn't anything that happened medically in their family that got by him, since their mother called when anyone got so much as a hangnail.

"You know why I'm here, sweetheart."

Alex sat on a stool by her kitchen bar, where she'd left a cup of tea. "Can I get you anything?"

"I got it." Cris pulled an unmarked tea bag out of the crock on the counter, opened the cupboard and got a mug, and checked the temperature of the tea kettle. He poured hot water over the bag and sat next to her.

"Smells good. What is it?" Cris asked.

"Chamomile and honey."

"Very nice." He breathed in the aroma.

Cristobal had made a name for himself in Northern Californian medical circles as a proponent of complementary alternative medicine. He trusted in the science of medicine while, at the same time, believing there were other methodologies that complemented what the American Medical Association deemed traditional. Chinese medicine, for example.

He believed things like acupuncture, cupping, and meditation increased chi—the life-giving, vital energy that unites body, mind, and spirit—to overcome illness, become more vibrant, and enhance mental capacity.

The research team he led at the medical startup he co-founded was focused on the genetic basis of aging. Cristobal believed that human life span could increase by decades if they could unlock the ability to feed the genes that caused aging.

"I'm not here to lecture you, Alex," he began. "But a mass is no more than a collection of cells that have adhered where they don't belong."

"You're saying I could've avoided surgery?"

"Not necessarily, but it is indicative of your body needing more than you're giving it."

"I thought I was pregnant."

Cristobal nodded.

"I see this as a sign."

"Of?"

"I don't belong with Maddox."

"I don't find that line of thinking particularly logic-based. Not remotely so."

Alex rolled her eyes and laughed. "Feeling's a feeling, Cris. Can't logic away feelings."

"How are you physically?"

"Wiped. The doc asked whether I experienced pain when I cut my finger. I told him I did, of course."

"This cut was much bigger, and not only superficial. He cut on the inside of your body, too."

"Essentially what he said. Is my surgery the only reason you're here?"

"Yes and no. I'm taking a long weekend because, like you, I'm wiped."

"You work way too much. Take some time for yourself. Maybe date a little."

"Mind your own business, Alex."

Looking more closely, Alex saw the dark circles under her brother's eyes and noticed his hair was peppered with more gray than the last time she'd seen him.

Of all her brothers, Cristobal was the most beautiful. She and her brothers had long, thin faces, like their mother, and dark brown hair that looked almost black. Cristobal and Gabe were the only two who got their father's hazel eyes; the rest got their mother's dark brown ones.

Cristobal's eyes were greener than Gabe's, more like Peyton's, and with his wavy hair, he looked more like a male model than a doctor.

He was in the middle of his residency at Stanford when their father died, and admitted struggling with a sense of guilt that he hadn't been able to save him. Something he would've called not particularly logic-based.

"Don't tell me to mind my own business. Tell me what's wrong."

"Nothing unusual. Working too many hours. Feeling pressure to produce results for the venture capitalists, even though they're not the ones pushing."

"Something else is bothering you, Cris."

"I'm worried about Gabe and Enzo. Something is going on at Los Cab."

"I've been worried about Enzo too. I don't know what Gabe's problem is."

"My take is Enzo is the one causing problems."

5

Naughton had Huck and Shazam saddled and ready to ride. Shazam was a purebred bay Leopard Appaloosa gelding with a bald face, four white socks, a black mane, and a salt and pepper tail. The horse looked small at a little under sixteen hands, standing next to Huck. He was Maddox's favorite horse to ride, especially when he rode with Alex.

"What's up?" Naughton asked once they were out on the trail.

"You heard about Kade's letter to Peyton?"

"That damn box."

"Crazy how it just kept showing up."

Naught shook his head. "That isn't what you wanted to talk about."

"I got my own letter from Kade."

Naughton looked away and didn't say anything.

"He left some property to me."

Why hadn't he thought this through, given more thought to how he'd tell his brother? If he were in

Naught's shoes, he'd sure as hell be wondering why Kade left property to Maddox and not anyone else.

"Yeah?"

"On Old Creek Road."

Naughton still hadn't looked at him. "I should've told you."

"Wait. What? You knew?"

Naughton nodded.

"I don't understand."

"I looked at the vineyards."

"What's there?"

"The vines are older than shit, but most are still viable."

"What percentage?"

Naughton shrugged. "Not sure. They're all pretty tired, but worth another look."

"What's there?"

"A lot."

"Did you know what he planned to do with it?"

Naughton shrugged.

"He said it was time I left Butler Ranch."

"He was so full of shit sometimes," Naughton laughed.

Maddox leaned up against a split-rail fence. "You don't think it's time for me to leave?"

"Why? The land is less than twenty miles from here."

"You think it's possible to handle both."

"I love this ranch, you know that…" Naught began. "But there's so much more we can grow there."

"Go on."

"Pinot Noir, for starters. Cab Franc, Petite Syrah."

They grew all of that except Pinot Noir at Butler Ranch, but Maddox knew what Naughton meant. None would ever be Butler Ranch signature wines. The ranch relied on the consistent income the flagship wines provided.

Buying more land adjacent to the ranch was impossible. All of it was owned by the Avilas and the Dunnings. The families had been in Paso Robles for generations, and just like the Butlers, there were sons, daughters, and grandchildren ready to pick up when the previous generation was ready to retire.

If they wanted to expand their production, try new varietals, experiment with rootstock, it had to be like the land on Old Creek Road.

"Why didn't he give it to both of us?"

"He did."

"What does that mean?"

"Two hundred for you, two hundred for me. There might be more if we want it."

"There's more?"

"The entire estate. All together maybe two hundred hectares. At one point, it was for sale."

Holy shit! Maddox's head was spinning. That amounted to almost five hundred acres.

"Why doesn't Da know this?"

"It wasn't between Kade and our parents; it was between us."

"Okay, why didn't I know?"

"He planned to tell you when he came back."

Maddox was afraid that was the case.

"Does it really matter, Mad?"

"Kade's letter said there was something more there that'll blow my mind. Is this it?"

Naughton laughed again. "Nah, there's somethin' else, but he made me swear to let you find it yourself." He shook his head. "So full of shit…"

"Where do we start?"

"Walk it."

"You said you should've told me. Why didn't you?"

"Doesn't matter."

"But you knew he bought it."

"I knew he owned it." Naughton hung his head, and the enthusiasm he'd been displaying dissipated.

"How?"

Naught shrugged his shoulders. "I didn't ask and he didn't offer."

Four hundred acres on Old Creek Road had to have gone for at least four million. What the hell had Kade been involved in? There was no way he pocketed that kind of money as a soldier.

Maddox had to wonder what else Kade had been hiding, and when it would surface.

—:—

"Hungry?" Cristobal asked.

"Always."

"Where to?"

"I don't care. Surprise me."

Cristobal drove to Moonstone Beach Road and pulled into the Sea Chest parking lot. The restaurant didn't take reservations and seated people first come, first served. The line on Friday night formed early. Depending on the season, there were people waiting as early as three in the afternoon.

Cris climbed out of the car and walked in through the back door of the restaurant. He came back out, a few minutes later, and motioned for Alex to follow.

"I forgot you used to date Stormy," she said as he guided her through the kitchen and into the oyster bar.

"Hotness has its perks." Stormy smiled and set menus in front of them. "How are you, sweetie?"

"I'm okay."

"If you need anything, you know my number."

"Thanks, Stormy."

She kissed Alex's cheek.

"How've you been?" he asked.

"Great. How about you? Found time for anyone special, Dr. Avila?"

"He works too much. No time for play. Right, Cris?"

When her brother scowled at her, Stormy looked back and forth between them and then shrugged her shoulders. "Alrighty, then." She smiled and walked away.

"Excuse me for a minute."

Alex nodded when Cris got up and walked to the back, where the restrooms were.

"Is this seat taken?" A man Alex didn't recognize sat in her brother's stool at the bar.

"It is."

He stood back up. "Damn, I would've loved to have dinner with you tonight."

Alex smiled. "Thanks," she murmured.

"Perhaps another time." The man handed her a card. "Call me. Anytime."

She studied the card. "Rory Calder. I'm Alex Avila." She held out her hand. "I know your wine well."

"Alex? This is great. I just saw Peyton, and she said you wouldn't be in until next week."

Cris came back from the men's room, and Alex introduced them. "You know Calder Wines, don't you?"

Cris nodded and invited Rory to join them. When he agreed, Cris motioned to Stormy, who brought another menu.

"Would it be better if we moved to a table, maybe something in the back?" Alex offered.

"No," Stormy and Cris said in unison.

"You'll…uh…be more comfortable here," Stormy stammered.

"What's up?" Alex asked Cris.

"Nothing. So, Rory, what brings you down to Cambria?"

"This one." He smiled at Alex. "Peyton, too."

"We only carry westside wines, Rory," Alex began.

"I know, and that's why I'm here. Calder Wines just bought Tablas Creek."

"I hadn't heard," she muttered, annoyed by how out of the loop she felt. "Bold move. Tablas Creek is huge." Alex and Peyton prided themselves on their insider knowledge of the Paso Robles wine region, but lately, neither had had their head in the game.

The previous owners of Tablas Creek were not well-liked in the valley or in the collaborative. The sons of Jean Lennoc, owner of the famous winery in Châteauneuf-du-Pape, had raised ire among the locals when they first purchased the land in the late eighties.

Their insistence on planting solely French clones left many of the old-school Paso Robles winemakers chilled. In 1990, the US Department of Agriculture stepped in and quarantined all of Lennoc's vines, slowly releasing them over the next two decades. The financial consequences must have been staggering, yet the Lennocs refused to give up. Evidently, whatever Calder had offered was worth their acquiescence.

"Not as big as what I've heard Butler Ranch is taking on. I can't believe they were able to snag part of the Hess estate."

Alex refused to ask Rory what he was talking about. Instead, she played it off as if she knew more than he did, raising her eyebrows and smiling.

"Did I hear Butler Ranch?" Maddox came around the corner of the oyster bar. "Hey, Alex." He walked straight over, put his arm around her, leaned in, and before she could turn away, planted a noisy kiss on her lips.

"Do you know Rory Calder?" asked Cris.

"Sure…uh…how've you been?"

"He was just commenting on your expansion," Alex quipped.

Maddox looked stunned. "Already?"

Rory shook Mad's hand. "Congratulations. Our family would've loved to get in on that property."

Alex continued the charade of knowing what they were talking about, grinning and nodding her head, while inside she seethed.

"Is this why you didn't want to move to a table in the back?" she whispered to Cris, who nodded his head.

"Is he here alone?"

Cris wouldn't look at her, but shook his head.

"Excuse me," she said to Rory and Maddox before she slipped from her seat and walked around the bar, toward the ladies room.

There was only one table in the back solely occupied, but clearly set for two. Alex didn't recognize the woman waiting for Maddox to return.

Her shoulder-length, bottle-blonde hair was perfectly coiffed, and her dagger-length nails were polished bright orange. The white denim jeans she wore looked painted on, and the tan hue of her skin was obviously from a tube of self-tanner. Her cell phone rested on the table, next to her place setting, and she was running her finger over it as though she was reading messages.

Alex approached the table. "You look so familiar, but I can't place where I know you from."

"I doubt we know each other…" the woman began, but was abruptly interrupted by Maddox's return.

"Alex." He grinned. "Have you met Lena Hess?"

"No, I haven't." Alex leaned forward to shake the woman's hand. When she presented a limp half-shake, Alex felt sick to her stomach. *One of those.*

Lena looked as uncomfortable as Alex felt. Her tan hue yellowed, and the look she gave Maddox screamed, *get me out of here.*

"I was just going to suggest we join you, Cris, and Rory," Maddox said, "but I wanted to be sure I wasn't interrupting anything."

"No more than I've interrupted you." Alex smirked.

"Good, then. Lena?" Maddox put his hands on the back of her chair.

"Where are we going?" she stammered.

"Into the oyster bar," Alex answered for Maddox. "My brother Cris and my friend Rory are waiting for us. Right, Maddox?"

"That's right. Stormy moved your things from the bar to the table in the front window."

"How thoughtful." Alex spun around, letting them follow her wake. Whatever the hell Maddox Butler was up to, she'd make him feel damn uncomfortable while he was at it.

—:—

Maddox sat between the two women, soaking in the jealousy seeping off Alex. It was obvious she didn't know Rory Calder as well as she pretended she did, which he and Cris appeared to find equally amusing. Lena and Rory, however, made eye contact several times. They acted as though they didn't know each other, but Maddox got the impression they were hiding the fact that they did.

"Were you aware Calder Wines purchased Tablas Creek?" Alex asked between spoonfuls of chowder.

"Congratulations," Maddox said to Rory. "We'll look forward to having a new member in the collaborative who understands the definition of the word."

Conversation continued primarily between Rory and Maddox, whose singular goal appeared to be to get as much information as he could about his rival.

"How many hectares will you plant this year?" Rory countered.

"None." Maddox took a big bite of garlic bread and turned to Alex. "We'll be lucky to be ready next year. Right, Al?"

"I have no idea, Maddox. What do you think, Lena?"

"That isn't my concern." She glared at Maddox. "Excuse me." She dabbed her lips while Maddox rose to get her chair.

When she stood, he leaned forward slightly as though he was inhaling her scent.

"Play nice," Maddox whispered in Alex's ear after Lena was out of hearing distance.

Alex ignored him. "Rory, did you have a chance to discuss scheduling a wine dinner when you saw Peyton?"

"She asked if I could stay in town tonight. She was going to see if you could come in for a brief meeting tomorrow."

"Have you made arrangements for a place to stay?"

"I haven't, and by the looks of the places I drove by on my way here, there aren't a lot of vacancies."

"Cris, are you planning to stay with me tonight?" Alex glanced to her left and could see steam coming out Maddox's nostrils.

"Well, I…"

"Not a problem," Maddox interrupted. "We have an apartment at the ranch that we keep for out of town guests. You can follow me back after dinner. We could even swing by Old Creek Road on our way."

"What about your date, Mad?" Alex asked.

Lena returned to the table before he could respond.

"Oh, honey," Lena oozed. "I'm not his date. I'm his roommate."

6

"Where did that come from?" Maddox asked Lena once they were in the parking lot.

"She was so territorial, I thought I'd dish it back at her. I hope I didn't spoil anything between you. Although, I noticed you didn't hurry to dispel any misunderstanding."

Maddox laughed. "Yeah," he muttered, looking toward the door of the restaurant, "I'll pay for that later."

"Sorry—"

"No apology necessary. As you said, I didn't exactly try to clear things up for her."

"I'm not really your roommate; I'm more of a tenant."

"You take your time. I'm in no hurry."

"You're sweet, Maddox, and I appreciate this."

He opened her door and waited while she climbed into her pearl-white Mercedes CLS400 Coupe.

"Goodnight, Lena. We'll chat tomorrow."

She waved and pulled out of the parking lot, leaving Maddox with a decision to make. Should he go back inside, in which case Alex would know he didn't leave with Lena?

He hated playing games with her, but it was the kind of thing they fell into easily. She should know he wouldn't be out with another woman, in the same way he knew she had no interest in Rory Calder.

Rory, however, was a different story. The man drooled every time Alex spoke. That's why he'd invited him to stay at Butler Ranch tonight—so he could make sure he wasn't within ten feet of her.

When Maddox turned to go back inside, it was just in time to see Rory slipping out the front door and into a car illegally parked in the loading zone. He must've decided he didn't need a place to stay after all, and as long as Alex wasn't with him, that didn't bother Maddox at all. There was something about the guy that rubbed him the wrong way. He couldn't say why he felt the way he did, but something told him Rory Calder was bad news.

When Maddox walked back inside, he didn't see Cris, but Alex was still at their table.

"Hey." He leaned down and put his arm around her shoulders.

"Where's your roommate? Got her motor running?"

"About that—"

"Save it, Maddox, I don't give a shit what you do or who you do it with."

"We both know you don't mean that, darlin'."

Out of the corner of his eye, Maddox saw Cris stop and talk to Stormy at the bar, buying him a few more minutes.

"Cris staying at your place tonight?"

"No, he's going to Los Cab."

"Good, I'll meet you there."

"Where?"

"Your place."

"What about Rory? I thought you two were going to bond over land purchases."

"Nah. He left. Must've gotten a better offer."

"I'm tired, Maddox. Let's do this another time."

"I don't know what you think we're going to be doing, but I'm tired too, Alex."

"Then, go home."

"I'm way too tired to drive all the way back to Adelaida Trail."

"Old Creek Road is about ten miles closer, and your roommate probably has the bed turned down in anticipation of your arrival."

Maddox leaned forward and covered Alex's mouth with his. The tip of her tongue teased his lower lip, so he gently bit down, capturing it between his teeth. She smirked as she pulled away from him.

"You hate staying at my place."

"Is that what you think?"

"No, Maddox, it's what I know. You've said it often enough."

"It's growing on me."

"Oh, really? When is the last time you stayed with me? Do you even remember?"

"Of course I do…" Maddox forgot what else he was going to say when he saw Cris heading toward them.

"I called Los Cab, so Mama's expecting me shortly."

Alex stood. "Let's get going, then."

Cris looked back and forth between them. "Maddox, can't you take Al home?"

"What? No, Cris—"

"You got it." Maddox put his arm around her waist. "See ya, Cris."

"See ya, Alex," said her brother, walking away and waving behind him.

"I'd prefer to be alone tonight, Maddox."

"No, you wouldn't."

She folded her arms and glared at him. "I'm serious."

He smiled and held the door open for her. When she shivered, he put his jacket around her shoulders, and then helped her climb into his truck.

—:—

He drove the two blocks to her house, pulled into her driveway, parked, and came around to open her door. She knew better than to open it herself. He'd scolded her for it so many times over the years.

"A lady waits for a gentleman to get her door, Alex," he'd admonish.

She teased him about it, but she loved it. The other men she dated never got her door.

"What are you up to?" she asked, digging for her keys. Where the hell had she put them? "Shit."

"What?"

"I left my keys in Cristobal's car."

Maddox walked over to the flower pot where she left her spare key, and picked up the rock it was hidden under.

"How do you know where I keep my key?"

He walked past her and unlocked the door.

"Mad, I asked you a question."

"One I shouldn't have to answer, but as I recall, you didn't remember much else about that night."

He held the door open and when she walked past him, leaned forward. "Did you, Alex?" he whispered.

She wanted to slam the door in his face, but he was too quick. He was already inside, looking in her refrigerator.

"What are you looking for? You just ate dinner."

"Somethin' to drink." Maddox pulled out the bottle of wine she'd opened the night before. "Your favorite," he smirked.

"Your favorite."

"Come on, Alex, you love my rosé. Admit it."

She did, and he was right. She loved its beautiful light coral hue and its aromas of strawberry, watermelon, and guava which led perfectly into a palate imparting tropical fruits, fresh citrus, and a bright and crisp minerality. She could drink it every day and never tire of it.

"Back to how I knew where you hide your spare key—"

Alex held up her hand. It wasn't necessary to skip back down the lane of that memory. Wine festival weekend had been known to get the better of everyone at some point in their lives. That year had been her turn. She'd had too much to drink and too little to eat. Instead of risking her life or anyone else's by attempting to drive home, she'd called Maddox. After that, she didn't remember much, until the next morning when she woke up with the worst hangover she'd ever had.

"You don't have to stay, Mad."

He poured two glasses of wine, but set them both on the counter and walked over to where she leaned up against it.

"Let me see." He tugged on her shirt and gently pulled it out from where it was tucked into her jeans.

"You can't see it."

"Of course I can."

Maddox unfastened her jeans and slid them off her hips along with her panties. When they fell to her ankles, he knelt in front of her, raised her feet, one by one, and tossed her clothes aside.

He leaned forward and sprinkled kisses across her belly, right above the scar that ran along her bikini line.

"Does it hurt?"

"Only when someone kisses it." She smiled.

"Who else has been kissing your scar, Al?" he asked as his lips trailed down to her thigh. "You're bare, darlin'."

"For the surgery," she whispered.

"I like it."

Alex rested her hands on Mad's shoulders. It was becoming increasingly more difficult for her to hold her own body weight the further his tongue explored.

Maddox stood and took her hand. "Come with me."

Her bedroom was a wreck, like it always was, but this was Maddox. He knew her, and didn't give a shit what her room looked like.

"Over here, baby." Mad opened the door and led her to the unmade bed. He threw back the tangled mess of sheets and blankets, and patted where he wanted her. When she rested flat on the mattress, he fluffed a pillow and put it under her head.

—:—

Each button on her shirt was a barrier to her skin that he released slowly, one by one. When it hung open, he pulled the cups of her bra down so her breasts spilled over.

Alex mewled softly, the way she always did when he had his hands on her body.

Her stomach was concave, pelvic bones protruding, which meant she wasn't eating enough. For twenty years, he'd watched her body mature—he knew every nuance.

The pale, strawberry-shaped birthmark on her inner thigh drew him in, and he trailed kisses across her sex. In all those years, Alex had never been bare. This was new skin for him to explore and learn.

He hated the angry red slash that marked her, not because of the way it looked, but because of the pain it gave.

"Sweet baby," he murmured, keeping his touch soft, his kisses light. Tonight wouldn't be about sex. Instead, he would nurture her, something Alex normally resisted. Her pain, her weariness, her insecurity, left her vulnerable enough that he could do this without her protests. He could be gentle with her, even though they both preferred a little edge to their sex.

"Close your eyes, Al. Relax. Let me love on you a little."

Her muscles tensed at the mention of the word they both refrained from using, but then released as his fingers kneaded her flesh.

When Brodie called to tell Maddox that they'd taken Alex to the hospital, he thought she'd lost their baby. *Their baby.* He'd gone from the guy who wasn't sure he'd ever marry, doubted he'd have kids, to the father of Alex's baby.

In the last four days, he found himself daydreaming about being a dad. When he found out Kade had left him the property on Old Creek Road, he'd let his thoughts drift to the home he'd build for himself, Alex, and their children.

He kissed her belly, where his child would've been, and then up to her breasts. He'd already imagined how Alex would look, breastfeeding their baby.

The thing that sucked the most was he couldn't tell Alex any of this. She'd freak and be more distant than she'd been the last few days.

It was unusual for Maddox to pursue Alex. She was the one who walked away, and she was the one who decided when she was ready to come back.

She had to have been thrown when he told her he was bringing her back here and spending the night. It was completely out of character for him. He knew instinctively that if Alex ever thought she had the upper hand, she'd lose interest in him completely. It was his remoteness, his strength, his steadfastness that kept her coming back.

The upper hand. When Brodie was trying to figure out his shit with Peyton, he told Maddox that he'd never been in a relationship with a woman who had the upper hand. Maddox had told him that was his first mistake, thinking there was an upper hand. But there was with him and Alex.

She was as confident as she was sheltered. Or because of it. The first word he thought of with Alex was fierce, although it was a close call between fierce and beautiful. And alluring. Captivating. Maddening. Fascinating and sublime. She was all of those things equally.

Alex was also timid, insecure, and filled with self-doubt. No one saw that side of her, not even Peyton. The bravado she showed the world masked what Maddox knew lay beneath. She needed someone stronger than her to feel safe in that persona.

The mistake so many made with people they considered strong was assuming they wouldn't feel the same kind of pain a person with more transparent feelings would. It couldn't be further from the truth. The strong just held it inside better.

When his father answered the door last year, and they were told Kade had been killed in action, Maddox had to get as far away from people as he could. He went out on the land, and roamed until he couldn't see light from any house. He sat on a rock and cried for his brother. He still did, but only out where no one could see or hear him. That was when he would rail at the heavens for taking Kade away from him—the one man Maddox knew was stronger than he was.

Alex's breathing evened, she'd drifted off to sleep. Maddox crept up the mattress so his body was next to hers. She turned in her sleep, and they spooned, her favorite way to sleep. Alex could sleep with her back to him because she trusted him to always keep her safe, even though she'd never admit it out loud.

—:—

Tree branches brushing against the bedroom window woke Alex, but it was the howling wind that kept her awake—that and Maddox being in her bed.

They hadn't talked about the pregnancy false alarm since her first day in the hospital. There were times she wanted to ask if he was relieved, but couldn't risk it. If he said he was, she might break down in front of him, and then he'd know her secret.

She'd wanted the baby that wasn't there. No one knew how badly, and no one ever would. Now she only felt an emptiness nothing could fill.

Why had she let herself think about a life with Maddox—having his child, telling him she loved him, and hearing him say it back to her? They'd never said those words, and now, they never would.

It was time to end things for good. They couldn't keep coming back to one another only to leave again. As long as they were on and off and on again, they wouldn't meet someone else, fall in love, and finally grow up.

The idea of not feeling his arms around her ever again hurt almost as bad as it did when she found out she wasn't pregnant.

Getting pregnant had never occurred to her. She'd been on the pill for years, and up until that one night, Maddox had always used a condom.

When she thought she was pregnant, she decided it was a sign. It had to mean she and Maddox were meant to be together. Now she knew better. No baby. No life with Maddox. What was he even doing here?

Tears slid down her cheeks, but soon it would be worse. She could feel it coming, and she wouldn't be able to stop it.

—:—

Maddox woke when Alex's body shuddered. At first he thought she was chilled, but soon he realized she was sobbing. He tightened his arms around her.

"Darlin', what's got you so sad?"

She shook her head, and her body convulsed. Maddox hadn't seen Alex cry this hard since her father died.

"Come on, baby. Tell me."

Alex buried her face in the pillow, and her sobs diminished. She slid out of the bed and went into the bathroom. When she returned, her eyes were red and puffy, but she'd stopped crying. She'd also put on a robe that she must've left in the bathroom.

"Alex?"

"I had a bad dream. It was nothing."

"What did you dream about, Al?"

"My dad. I miss him."

Maddox sensed she was lying, but he couldn't call her out on it. What would he say without divulging his own secret? Alex, are you sad about not being pregnant? Because I am.

"It's the anesthesia. Cristobal told me it would take a while for my body to shake its effects."

Maddox raised an eyebrow, but let it go. "Come back to bed." He reached for her, but she stepped back.

"I'll make some coffee." The words trailed as she walked out of the bedroom.

Maddox pulled on his jeans and joined her in the kitchen.

"We need to talk, Maddox," she began.

What was this? Alex didn't talk; she left.

7

Maddox drove home, still shell-shocked. He was the one who always wanted Alex to talk more, but now that she had, he regretted it.

She told him, in no uncertain terms, that she was ready to move on. He was her high school crush, and it was time they let each other go.

If she hadn't been so convincing, he might've tried to argue, but her words were clear and concise. There was no hesitation in her voice, no hint that this was the same Alex who might say it was over but would eventually come back.

He had an ache in his chest, the same one he felt whenever he thought about Kade. It was finality. Kade was gone forever, and while Alex still walked the earth, she was gone from him forever too.

He never thought he'd see this day, and that it came so close on the heels of them having a tie that would have kept them together forever, made it harder to accept.

It wasn't as though he could bury himself in wine-making and push his pain and disappointment aside; this was the slowest time of the year for him.

In June and July, Brodie was the only one of them who was busy. The early summer months were for selling wine, attending festivals, making contacts. Maddox would participate, but only when Brodie asked him to.

It was the same for Naughton. The vineyards needed his attention, but only to monitor the grape growth and keep an eye on things like pest infestation or mold.

If there was ever a time for the two of them to get started on the Old Creek Road property, it was now. A little back-breaking work might help him sweat away some of his anger and frustration over Alex. That was the only downside to starting this project in June. Daytime temperatures would be scorching.

He'd call Naught, but he'd be in the vineyard this early, so he decided to get some breakfast before driving home. Instead of going somewhere in Cambria or driving all the way to Paso Robles, Maddox stopped in Harmony. There were ten houses, one winery, and one restaurant in the little town, and the people who lived there liked it that way.

He parked a couple of doors down from Sadie's Diner, and cut the engine. Before he climbed out, something caught his eye. He blinked a few times at what he saw in the mirror. Damn if the guy walking across the road, a few hundred feet back, didn't look just like Kade.

Maddox jumped out and slammed the door behind him. The man must've gone into one of the houses because he was no longer on the road. Mad walked down that way anyway, even though there was no reason for him to. Kade was dead, and if he caught up to the guy he just saw, he'd think he was a whack-job. Maddox turned back around and went in the front door of Sadie's.

He sat at the counter, still shaken. How could anyone look so much like his brother? Same height, same build, even walked the same as Kade. Granted, he was pretty far away, but the cadence was so similar.

After his ma had the heart attack, he heard that Peyton had dreamed Kade came and talked to her, so had his mother. Maddox thought it was a little weird, but now he wondered if the same thing had just happened to him. Was he dreaming? If he was, he'd give anything to wake up, because then it would mean the conversation he'd had with Alex was just a nightmare.

"Look who's darkenin' my door this mornin'." Sadie came out of the kitchen and kissed his cheek. "How the hell are ya, Maddox?"

"Been better, Sadie."

"I hear ya, honey."

Maddox wasn't sure what Sadie meant, other than maybe her life wasn't any better than his at the moment. There'd been a time when he and Sadie tangled a few sheets, and she was a fine-looking woman, but he wasn't feeling it for her today. Maybe it was too soon; Alex's words had barely sunk in. Marry that with him thinking he just saw Kade, and Maddox wondered if being out in the hot sun later was such a good idea. He was already feeling a little delirious.

—:—

Just because Peyton was with Brodie, didn't mean Alex couldn't text her, did it? When Peyton was with Lang, Alex called whenever she wanted. He was never home anyway.

When Peyton was with Kade, Alex kept her distance. She knew Peyton would only be MIA for a short while, and then it would be time for Kade to leave on his next mission, and she and Peyton would have more time to hang out.

Brodie was different. He'd be with Peyton every chance he could, and he'd never be deployed. Was work the only place she'd see her best friend?

Whatcha' doin'? She texted.

Just got to Stave.

Be right in.

Thank goodness, Peyton was at Stave. Even if she didn't work all day, Alex would still have some time to tell her what she'd just done.

Alex parked her car behind the building and took a few deep breaths. She and Maddox had been apart before, after a fight, or when he was just being an asshole and she didn't want to be around him. This felt different, though. This was forever, and as hard as it would be for her to have enough self-control to stay away from him, her future depended on it. The ache she felt inside would go away. In a few days, she'd be over Mad-man Butler and ready to move on.

Thinking she was pregnant, even for a few short weeks, made her view her life in a different way than she ever had before.

If she wanted a life like Peyton was going to have with Brodie, and she did, she had to break out of the Maddox paradigm and find someone she could make a life with. If Maddox Butler wanted something more than sex with her, he would've said so years ago.

Brodie was the only Butler boy who was settling down. Alex doubted Maddox or Naughton ever would. If he'd lived, Kade wouldn't have either, even though, at one time, Alex thought he might propose to Peyton.

When she walked in the back door of Stave, she heard Brodie's voice coming from the bar. He and Peyton were talking to someone about Butler Ranch wine. He sounded so much like Maddox that, for a minute, she considered turning around and going home.

"Look who's here." Brodie was the first to see her and greeted her with a hug.

Peyton was right behind him.

"Why does it feel as though I haven't seen you at all, Alex?"

"A lot's been happening. You're engaged...and other stuff."

"What other stuff?"

"Nothing major," she lied through her teeth. It didn't get much more major in Alex's life; Maddox had been an integral part of it since she was a teen-ager. She shook her head, trying to shake off the tears that threatened.

"Be right back," she said to Peyton and went into the restroom.

"Where'd Brodie go?" she asked when she returned.

"He just dropped me off. He's going back to the house, and then he and the boys are adventuring."

"Do you want to go with them? I can cover."

"Heck, no." Peyton walked over and hugged her again. "I miss you like crazy, Alex. We need to catch up."

"I was thinking the same thing. You go first."

Peyton pulled a stool from around the corner of the bar. "Have a seat, Alex, and tell me what's going on."

"I might as well be in a coma compared to what's happening in your life. You're engaged. You're pregnant. Tell me how he proposed. I'm dying to hear the story."

"Nope, you're not distracting me. I'm not saying another word until you tell me what's up."

The people who had been in the tasting room left, and for now, they were alone. Alex might as well tell

Peyton now. Saturdays were always busy, and soon they wouldn't have a chance to talk.

"I ended things with Maddox," she began. "It was time."

"What happened?"

"Nothing really. Or maybe something huge…I decided I want more."

"More?"

"You know, what you have. A husband, a family, a future. I want that, Peyton."

"Did you tell Maddox that's what you wanted?"

Alex shook her head. "It isn't what he wants."

"Did he tell you that?"

"Sure did." Over the course of the last twenty years. Peyton studied her. "I'm surprised."

"At what?"

"That Maddox told you that."

"Don't be. Mad and I were friends with benefits, an expression I hate, but in this case, one that accurately describes our relationship."

"It's more than that, Alex. It's so obvious whenever the two of you are together."

"We're comfortable, that's all it is. I grew up with Maddox. If we hadn't had sex, he'd be like a brother to me."

"Ew."

"Right? Can we please change the subject? Tell me how Brodie proposed."

Peyton told Alex about the letter from Kade, and the ring, and how it all fell together so perfectly, as though it had been scripted.

"I'm sure Maddox told you about his letter," said Peyton.

"What? No, I don't know anything about another letter."

"You know about the Old Creek Road property, though, right?"

"That the Butlers bought it? I surmised that from the conversation between Mad and Rory last night."

"No, Alex. The Butlers didn't buy it. Kade did. And he left it to Maddox."

"You're kidding?" Alex did a mental calculation. "Where did Kade get that kind of money?" As soon as she said it, she wished she hadn't. Peyton looked haunted.

"I don't know," she murmured. "I don't want to think about it."

Alex nodded. This was huge, and Maddox hadn't mentioned anything about it. It was another sign he didn't want their relationship to change.

"Not just Maddox, though," Peyton continued. "Naughton, too. Together they own four hundred acres."

If Alex had taken a drink of the wine in front of her, she would've spit it all over the bar. Four hundred acres? How in the hell had Kade pulled that off?

"Did Laird and Sorcha help?"

"Brodie doesn't think so. They said they knew nothing about it."

"Maybe Kade robbed an Afghani kingdom no one knew about."

Peyton laughed, but Alex saw the worry in her eyes. Nobody came up with that kind of cash overnight.

—:—

Maddox called Naughton on his cell and asked if they could meet on Old Creek Road so he didn't have to drive all the way back to Butler Ranch. Naught told him he could be there in a couple of hours. While he waited, Maddox went exploring.

The severe drought the region had experienced over the course of the last few years took its toll. The earth was dry and desolate-looking, and the vines would look dead to the untrained eye.

Maddox parked near a single-story house not far from the entrance to the estate. The Mercedes was parked out front.

Last night, he and Lena had sat on the boardwalk overlooking Moonstone Beach before going into the restaurant. She told him that, at one point, her father had planned to expand winemaking at the ranch. When her mother was diagnosed with Parkinson's disease, that plan dried up like the land around it.

Lena had been living in Santa Barbara up until about five years ago when her mother's condition worsened. She sold her house and moved north in order to help her father.

Two years ago, her mother passed away, and her father moved away from the ranch, not wanting any part of it. Lena stayed, not knowing what to do next with her life.

When she asked if she could stay in the house a little while longer, Maddox told her she could stay as long as she wanted.

It would take three years, at least, for Naught and him to restore the vineyards. He didn't need to live here to do that, so he wasn't in a hurry to move out of his house on Butler Ranch.

Instead of knocking on the door of the house, Maddox followed a path that went through the trees.

Every footstep he took on this land brought another question about Kade. If he hadn't died, what had he planned to do with the acreage? Had he planned to live here with Peyton and her boys?

So many other questions plagued him. Why had it taken the lawyers so long to get in touch with his parents? Why had the lawyers called his parents instead of him? Why hadn't Naughton told him about the property? Kade had been dead for a year and four months.

Rather than roaming farther, Maddox turned around. He and Naught agreed to meet where he'd parked, and his brother should be there soon. He'd wait in the shade under one of the oak trees that lined the banks of the creek.

Between his conversation with Alex, and then seeing his brother's *doppelganger* in Harmony, he needed a rest alongside the water. Maybe its flow would ease the ache he felt deep in his soul.

He must've fallen asleep because the sound of his brother's motorcycle jarred him awake. The vintage BMW was worth a fortune, yet Naughton rode it around the hills of wine country like a dirt bike.

A thin layer of dry dirt from his nap by the creek clung to him like film. Maddox stood and swatted at his jeans to brush it off.

"See?" Naughton said, as though the dirt held the answer to a mystery.

"See what?"

"It's good stuff. Dryer than the Sahara, but it's what's in the soil that makes it stick."

Maddox's degree was in the science of enology—winemaking. Naughton was the environmental scientist. He specialized in viticulture, but it was the rest of his training that would help them figure out how to make something grow on the neglected land.

"Follow me." Naughton led him over rolling hills, pointing out different vineyards and what had been planted in them. They crested a hill and a grove of trees.

"Get ready," Naughton told him.

The trees gave way to a view that brought Maddox to his knees. Before him was the majestic Pacific Ocean, one hundred and eighty degrees of the most magnificent view he'd ever seen. Even the view on the south side of the highway that looked out over Morro Bay wasn't as breathtaking as this.

"Is this what Kade said I'd discover?"

Naughton shook his head and motioned for Maddox to follow. The land had a drastic slope on the western side, but in this case, that was a very good thing. It made hiking difficult, but the amount of vineyard area that would directly benefit from the warmth of the sun and the coolness of the ocean breezes, was more than he could've dreamed existed in this part of the country. These were among the best growing conditions he'd ever seen for Pinot Noir.

"Come on," Naught hollered. "Keep up."

His brother was a ways ahead of him, but Maddox refused to hurry. He was tempted to sit where he stood and simply watch the deep blue water, which looked almost black from this distance, flow to the shore and back out again.

The water looked calm from here, although he guessed the crashing waves were easily over ten feet, maybe more than twenty. He closed his eyes and breathed in the salty air, wishing Kade had shown him this when he was still alive so they could've enjoyed this moment together. He opened them and looked at the sky, a much lighter blue than the ocean, but no less vivid. The prevailing winds moved the billowing clouds farther inland quickly. Maddox shielded his eyes from the sun and saw Naughton standing below, looking up at him.

"Are you coming?" he shouted, sounding more like his little brother of thirty years ago.

Maddox took one more deep breath, wishing Alex were with him today—wishing she'd been at his side the first time he saw this view. There was a big rock near the edge of what had once been rows of vineyard. He picked it up and brought it back to the place he'd been standing, vowing to bring her back with him so she could see the view from the same perspective he had.

"There's more down here," Naughton shouted.

"Okay, okay." Maddox laughed and made his way down the steep terrain. When he got to the place where Naughton waited, his brother pointed to the right. Maddox followed and saw what Naught was in such a hurry for him to see. A cave, and not a small one. This cave was man-made, like the ones on Butler Ranch. No telling what treasures it held.

"What's in there?" Maddox asked.

"Dunno."

"Hey, Naught, why'd you wait? Why not tell me about this land right after Kade died?"

Naught turned his back to Maddox and rubbed the back of his neck. It was a tell. All of his brothers did it when they were stressed.

"Naught?"

"I can't answer that."

"What the hell? Kade's dead. The decision whether to tell me or not was yours."

When Naughton turned back around, Maddox saw the sadness in his brother's eyes. "It's the way he wanted it, Maddox. I'm sorry."

8

Two more days and Alex could escape. The walls of the small seaside village where she lived and worked were closing in on her. Butler Ranch seemed to be on the tip of everyone's tongue. If it wasn't tourists talking about their fabulous wines, it was locals wanting to know what she and Peyton knew about the Old Creek Road property.

If one more person asked her about it, she'd scream. The whole thing pissed her off. Every time someone asked, she was reminded that Maddox hadn't told her anything about it.

"I'm gonna take a break."

Peyton was sitting in the office and waved when Alex went past. "Have a good walk."

The sidewalks of the village were crowded with tourists, so Alex went behind the buildings to the end of Main Street, and cut through the tall grasses until she came to the highway.

Farther south it was known as Pacific Coast Highway, but this stretch was known as Cabrillo Highway. It ran parallel to the coast, from Santa Barbara to San Francisco, straight through Big Sur.

A massive rock slide had closed the highway north of Cambria months ago, and there was no word on when it might reopen. The only other way to get to Big Sur was to drive inland, take Highway 101 north, and then go back out to the coast near Carmel.

It was a shame because her favorite escape, Post Ranch Inn, was in Big Sur. With only two days off, driving the long way would eat up too much of her time. The only other way to get there was by helicopter.

Damn Maddox. If he only wanted her the way she wanted him, if only he could love her, they could have such a wonderful life. She'd work by his side through the busiest times of the year at the winery. From harvest to crush to fermentation to bottling, they'd be together, doing something they were both born to do. And then, when things quieted down, he could fly them to the inn where they'd spend a relaxing and romantic week.

She'd talk him into doing yoga with her at dawn, and then they'd swim in the infinity pool that looked as though they could swim right out into the ocean.

They'd get massages, and at night, gaze at the stars. In between they'd ravish each other's bodies like no one else could.

Maddox taught her how to experience pleasure like many didn't know existed. He knew every inch of her body, where she was ticklish, and the places that made her body hum.

No other lover she'd had came close to bringing her the pleasure Maddox did. Not that there were many. What was the point when she knew she'd only end up frustrated, wanting Maddox more than ever?

How could she find someone like him? Place an ad? Experienced lover wanted. Must strike the perfect balance between rough and gentle. Know the edge of pain, the kind that brings pleasure. Willing to learn what every gasp or breath means. To learn the very moment she reached the crescendo, and softly play her back down. She doubted any such man existed.

Traffic was heavy on the highway, so it took her a few minutes to cross to where she could catch the trail that would lead her down to Moonstone Beach. There was someone there she needed to talk to.

—:—

"Where do they end?"

Maddox and Naughton had been exploring the caves carved into the side of the hills for over an hour. Each time they turned a corner, thinking they'd come to the end, the pathway would make another turn and lead to more rooms.

There was no mistaking the areas that were used to store barrels. The smell of the wine-soaked wood permeated the air, and with no way to escape, it lingered. It was a smell not all found pleasant, but Maddox loved it.

He loved everything about wine barrels—their smell, their texture, the flavors different types or ages of barrels imparted in the wine.

When Alex and Peyton got the okay from Peyton's father to expand the Wolf Family Vintners tasting room into something that would showcase all the westside wineries, they'd talked to Maddox about a name.

"How many wineries are in the collaborative?" he asked, already knowing the answer.

Alex thought about it for a minute, and then smiled. "It's perfect."

"Thirty-one?" Peyton asked.

"How many staves in a barrel?" Alex grinned.

"Oh. It *is* perfect."

An average barrel was made of thirty-one strips of wood, called staves. The collaborative may grow or shrink, but Stave would always represent each strip of wood that made the barrel whole.

The smell of wine-soaked wood grew stronger, and Maddox followed the scent. Around the next corner was a door, many of the rooms had them. This door was locked, but he knew damn well there were barrels of wine inside. How many, what was in them, and where they came from was a mystery.

What he wouldn't do was break the door down. If he had to bring a locksmith all the way out here, he would, but first he'd ask Lena. Maybe she knew about the wine in the caves, and if she didn't, maybe she'd seen keys laying around and didn't know what they were for.

Maddox had asked Naughton at least three times if their latest discovery was what Kade had alluded to in his letter. This time, Naught beat him to it.

"This isn't it either, but look." Not far from the locked door, there was a key sitting on a ledge.

His hands shook as he tried it, almost too excited to go inside the room. The key turned, and he heard the click. Naughton shone the light from his phone into the room, and it was nearly full of barrels. By rough count, almost one hundred.

How anyone had gotten that many barrels in here was confounding. There had to be another entrance. Transporting this number of barrels would've been treacherous the way they came in.

Maddox made his way around the crowded room. Off to the side was a shelf that held the exact thing he was hoping to find—a thin glass tube, known as a thief, which would allow him to taste what was in the barrels.

He gently removed the bung plug from the top of the barrel and lowered the thief into the wine. Maddox didn't need to see what he was tasting. In fact, he preferred not to. This would be all about taste, and he couldn't wait.

The aroma wafting from the barrel gave him his first clue. If this was what he thought it was, it meant there were vines somewhere on this property that were priceless.

—:—

Alex sat on the beach and let the sand run through her fingers. Her papa was here, in this sand. This was where she and her brothers had brought his ashes.

When they were growing up, he brought her and her brothers here a lot. When the weather was warm, he'd bring them here to play in the water. When one of them was faced with a big decision, he'd bring them here to walk on the beach and let the endless waves crashing on the shore help them figure things out. Sometimes they'd just sit and watch the otters play.

When he died, she'd turned to Maddox. He held her when she cried, and when he did, she could feel her father's arms around her.

Maddox had been the one responsible for the truce that had ended the bitter feud between their families. If only it could have happened while her papa was still alive.

He and Laird Butler had so much in common. Instead of shunning one another, what could they have accomplished if they'd worked together?

Her oldest brother took over the winery when their father passed, but it was the Butler family who made sure the harvest was brought in, the grapes were crushed, the wine was made and bottled. Without their help, they would have lost a year's production, or more.

She'd walked the vineyard then, talking to her papa up in heaven. "Can you see what they've done for us? They saved us."

She wished, so often then, that her father had known Maddox and what a fine man he was. What a shame that his pride had stood in the way of what might have been.

If he were still alive, would the feud have ended? Would Maddox have found a way to bring their two families together?

"Is it my fate to be alone because no man will ever mean as much to me as Maddox? I think I love him, Papa."

She looked at her phone and realized she'd been gone a lot longer than she meant to be. Time to brush away her tears, stand up straight, and show the world strong-Alex, not falling-apart-because-she's-heartbroken-Alex.

—:—

Maddox closed his eyes and let the wine linger on his palate. It exuded power and elegance. It was dense, yet focused with bright, fresh characters. There was plenty of ripe blue and red fruit accompanied by what?

The flavors overwhelmed him—mocha, carob, butterscotch, and toast. There were even hints of dried herb and rose petal.

The wine's lengthy tannins complemented the underlying intense fruit. This was a wine that could age for years and still exhibit youthful characteristics. It may very well be the best Cabernet Sauvignon he'd ever tasted.

Something was wrong, though. This wine wasn't very old. It couldn't be. It also couldn't have been made from fruit grown in the vineyards outside these caves. Those vines had been dormant far too long. Where had this wine come from, and who made it?

"This isn't it either," Naught said before Maddox took another taste of the mystery wine.

Each thing he discovered was more fascinating, and yet none of it was what Kade had alluded to in his letter. What else could there be?

—:—

Alex hadn't been back at Stave fifteen minutes when Gabe threw the back door open. "Where's Maddox?

"Hi, Gabe, how are you?"

"Cut the crap, Alex. Where's Maddox?"

She folded her arms. "I don't know. Why?"

"I need to find him, or Naughton. Either one."

"What's your problem?"

"I need to talk to him. Where is he?"

Peyton motioned toward the tasting room, where Sam was helping customers.

"Come with me." Alex pulled Gabe out the back door and stood with her hands on her hips. "Tell me why."

"Do you know where he is or not?"

"Stop yelling at me."

"For Christ's sake, Alex. I'm not yelling at you."

Alex looked left and right. "I'm the only one here, and you're yelling. Which means you're yelling *at me*. If you don't stop, I'm not going to tell you a damn thing about Maddox Butler."

Gabe paced in the parking lot, running his hand through his thick head of dark hair. Like Cristobal, his was peppered with more gray than she remembered. Gabe was forty, and Cristobal was thirty-eight. Wasn't that early to turn gray?

"You need to relax." Alex tried to put her hand on Gabe's shoulder, but he swatted it away.

Alex spun around to go back inside, but Gabe caught her arm.

"Wait." He lowered his voice, but the grip he had on her arm made her uncomfortable.

"Let go of me," she sneered.

He let go, leaned up against his truck, and looked at the ground. "I'm sorry. If you talk to him or Naughton, can you ask one of them to get in touch with me?"

"Tell me why it's so important."

"None of your concern."

"I'll be right back. I'll let Peyton know I'm leaving, and then you can tell me what's going on."

Peyton was waiting when Alex came inside. "What's up?" she asked.

"I don't know. Gabe is acting very odd. He keeps saying he needs to talk to Maddox, if not him, Naughton."

"Hmm."

Alex nodded and opened the back door.

"Shit. He's gone."

She called Gabe's cell, and it went straight to voicemail. Next she called Enzo, and it went straight to voicemail too. The same thing happened with Trev. She didn't expect him to answer, though. He handled sales for Los Caballeros and, at this time of year, was quite busy. The only person she hadn't called was Maddox.

Peyton called Brodie, who had no idea why Gabe would need to talk to his brothers.

"I don't want to call Maddox."

"Brodie said he couldn't reach him anyway, or Naughton. He tried, but neither answered."

"It seems like Gabe is mad about something. Is it me, or did you get that impression too?"

"Maybe. Whatever it is, it's odd."

She'd hoped she was making more of it than it was, but if Peyton was getting a vibe too, then something was up.

So much for escaping for a couple of days.

9

This was feeling too familiar. Alex had been a little girl when the feud between her father and Laird Butler started. The stories she heard about how it started didn't make sense to her.

She'd always believed her father to be an honorable, good, and decent man. His accusing Laird Butler of paying off wine judges just because her family's wine hadn't medaled didn't sound like him. There had to have been more to the story. Maybe he'd had proof of his accusation, and that was why he was intransigent about reconciling with the Butler family.

***

When Alex was growing up, her older brothers warned her and their younger siblings not to mention the Butler name in front of their father. She respected her parents, so she never did, not even to ask her mother what had happened.

It wasn't until she and her cousin Bianca started high school that she paid any attention to the Butler boys, or any boys, for that matter.

Alex grew up with six brothers, and she was one of them. Everything they did, she did. It didn't matter whether it was riding their horses, fishing, playing sports, or playing cards—Alex was one of the guys. The summer before her freshman year, her mother encouraged her to spend more time with Bianca and less time trailing after her brothers.

Bianca had two older sisters and no brothers. She encouraged Alex to dress more femininely, which she had no interest in doing.

"You don't have to go all girly-girly, but how about somewhere between that and how you are now?"

"How am I now?" Alex asked.

"With your short hair and flat chest, most people think you're a boy. No guy will ever ask you out, Alex."

Alex didn't care—until she saw Maddox Butler for the first time. She and Bianca went to the county fair, and there he was. He took her breath away, and when he looked at her, he didn't even see her.

Between that summer and the next, Bianca helped her pick out clothes that would flatter her figure, and Alex let her hair grow longer.

Peyton went to a private school in San Luis Obispo, but in the summer, she and Alex were almost inseparable. Bianca took the two best friends shopping, showed them how to use makeup, and encouraged them to wear clothes that were more flattering.

Fortunately for her, that same summer, her body decided to play along. Alex was still tall and thin, but she was no longer flat-chested.

By the next summer, she noticed more guys checking her out, and had even been asked out a couple of times. She turned them down, though. There was only one guy she was interested in.

Alex had seen him at school last year, but not very often. He was a senior, and she was a freshman, and when she passed him in the hall, he still looked right through her.

She became obsessed with getting him to take notice, knowing full well that if he did, there were only two possible outcomes. He might not want anything to do with her once he knew she was an Avila. And if he was interested in her, and her brothers found out, Maddox might not live to see his first day of college.

Opening night of the county fair, Alex and Bianca were standing near the entrance, waiting for friends, when she saw Maddox walk in with his brother. For the next two hours, they followed the brothers everywhere they went, until he finally noticed her.

Every dream of him she'd had came true that night. He not only kissed her, he kept kissing her—for two hours.

Maddox ignited feelings in Alex she hadn't known existed. Every part of her tingled when his lips met hers.

"Give me your mouth," he demanded.

She had no idea what he meant until he grasped her chin and ran his tongue over her lips. She gasped when his tongue met hers.

"That's my girl," he moaned. His hands ran over her body and gripped her behind, pulling her closer to him.

"You feel me, Alex Avila?" he'd asked.

She had, and it excited and terrified her equally. He backed off then, but didn't stop kissing her. It was the best night of her life, and after it was over, she didn't see or speak to him for another three years.

Maddox went to UC Davis, she knew that much, but it wasn't until the summer after she graduated from high school that she heard he was home for the summer. She saw him a lot, but neither acknowledged the other if they were with their family.

On a particularly hot day in June, Alex and Bianca spent the day at Lake Naco. She was walking into the water when she saw him on a boat that was pulling up to the dock. Their eyes were riveted until Maddox jumped into the water from the side of the boat. He swam underwater and slid up her body to the water's surface.

"You feel me, Alex?" he'd said again that day.

A few weeks later, Maddox took her virginity. She'd been determined he would, since the day at the lake. In the same way he taught her to kiss, he taught her body how to respond to his.

***

Sex with him was incendiary. Every touch lit her on fire. He was demanding, and she loved it. He knew exactly how to set her off, like no one had since.

Alex doubted she'd ever find a man who did it for her like Maddox. But she needed more than mind-blowing sex. She needed love, and that wasn't something Maddox would ever be able to give her.

—:—

It took Maddox and Naughton an hour to make their way out of the caves. They went back and checked other rooms they'd passed with closed doors, but they didn't find any more barrels of wine. There was evidence that someone had been in the caves recently, though.

"What do you make of this?" Maddox asked.

"Someone's storing wine here."

"Who?"

"Maybe someone with a bond issue."

In order to legally make and sell wine, wineries had to take out bond coverage, which was essentially an insurance policy required by the feds, which covered a winery's annual excise tax liability.

Calculating that tax liability wasn't an easy thing to do. It took looking at the total volume in gallons of wine that a winery may potentially have stored on their site during any given month of the year. To further complicate things, that total volume had to be broken out by tax class, which was determined by each wine's alcohol content.

If a winery vastly underestimated their production, or if what they produced was significantly different in terms of alcohol content, and they didn't bring their bond up to meet the changes in production, they could face stiff fines and penalties, including loss of their license to sell the wine they produced.

Naughton's guess that it might be someone with a bond issue made sense. The barrels were unmarked, and obviously whoever put them there, needed to store them somewhere they wouldn't be found.

"Heard any rumblings about anyone in trouble?" Maddox asked.

"Brodie or Alex would hear before we would."

Brodie had essentially been out of the wine business for the past six months. Which left Alex. Maddox wasn't in a position to call her at all, let alone call her only to ask about wine industry gossip.

The number of barrels stored in the caves was worth a substantial amount of money. Whomever they belonged to would be back. Since he and Naughton planned to be here every day for the next month, analyzing the vineyards and formulating a plan to get them back into production, eventually, whomever the wine belonged to would show up, and they'd get their answer.

—:—

"I'm going home," Alex told Peyton.

"Good. We're fine here, and you don't want to do too much too soon. Get some rest."

The doctors had told Alex not to resume what she considered "normal activity" for four to six weeks. Her surgery was eleven days ago. She had a long way to go before she felt *normal* again. Although, with Maddox out of her life for good, what would normal feel like?

When Stave first opened, she walked to the tasting room and home every night. Life was simpler then, for both her and Peyton. Alex couldn't remember the last time she'd walked to work. It had to have been a couple of years at least, and yet, when she walked to Moonstone Beach earlier in the day, she'd been within two blocks of home.

Walking would be good for her, and she'd make it a point to do it more often. In fact, once she got home, she'd take another walk on the beach and talk to her papa again.

Being tired wasn't the only reason she left Stave. Gabe's behavior was so odd, something had to be wrong. She wished he, Enzo, or Trev would call her back, so she'd stop worrying.

Of the three, she was closest to Enzo and Trev, who were two years older and younger than Alex, respectively. Enzo looked out for her, and she looked out for

Trev. That's the way it worked in the Avila family; the older looked after the younger.

She'd be more upset if she'd told those two it was urgent they get back to her, but she'd only told them to call as soon as they had a chance.

Unlike the Butler boys, none of her brothers lived at Los Caballeros Ranch. There had been a guest house on the property at one time, but it had burned to the ground before Alex was born.

Gabe, Enzo, and Trev lived on their own in Paso Robles. Cristobal lived in Palo Alto, and her two youngest brothers shared a house in downtown PR, but they were almost never there. The rodeo circuit kept them on the road most of the year.

—:—

It had been a long, damned day, and Maddox was beat. It began shortly after sunrise, with Alex telling him they were done. This time, instead of just walking away, she'd told him straight out. It felt different because it was different.

Then, before breakfast, he could've sworn he saw his dead brother. And lastly, he roamed the land that same brother had left him, and explored wine caves unlike any he'd ever seen, including those on Butler

Ranch. Someone was storing barrels containing some of the best wine he'd ever tasted in those caves.

He closed his eyes, knowing he'd be asleep in minutes, hoping tonight he wouldn't dream about Kade or Alex.

—:—

Alex drifted off with the television on and her phone next to her. When she woke up at three a.m., there still were no calls from her brothers, and an infomercial blared on the flat screen.

Worse, what had jarred her awake in the first place, was a dream. In it, she and Maddox were walking along Moonstone Beach—and he was holding their baby.

It hadn't been twenty-four hours, yet her body yearned for his as though it had been months since she'd felt his touch. These feelings were easier to push away when she was mad at him about something.

Rolling to her side, Alex set her phone on the nightstand, but then picked it up and took one more look. Nothing. No texts, no calls, no messages.

She swiped to her photos and looked at the one that always came up first. It was a shot of Maddox, just his face and a little bit of his chest. Even his shoulders were cropped out of the image. He was looking straight into the camera; that's why she loved the photo so much. It felt as though he was looking right at her.

Alex ran the tip of her finger over his thick beard, his lips, and then down, to where the image ended. She'd never forget the day she took the photo, and if she closed her eyes, she could remember exactly what it would've looked like had she not focused on his face. He stood before her, naked, that day, daring her to take his photo.

She could see it in his eyes, the smirk, the laugh, the dare. She snapped so many images, but this was the best. It was one of the last ones she took before she'd erupted in giggles as Mad tried to pry the phone from her hand to see if she'd met his dare.

She had, but he deleted the one that showed him in all his glory. What she'd give to have that photo now.

When her phone pinged, she dropped it on the bed, as though it was burning hot.

10

Why was it when he was most tired, he couldn't sleep? Maddox tossed and turned all night. Along with replaying his conversation with Alex, he couldn't get the image of the man on the street in Harmony out of his head.

In both cases, he wished he'd acted. With Alex, he should have swept her up, tied her to the bed, and forced her to tell him again it was over. She wouldn't have been able to. Her body was his, and they both knew it. If he had his hands on her, Alex turned to putty.

Why was it so damn hard for him to tell her he wanted her to move in with him because he wanted her? It had nothing to do with her being pregnant. He needed her. Not one week out of every three or four, but always. Every day.

If Kade were still alive, that's whom he'd talk to. There had been many nights when they'd message back and forth. His three in the morning was Kade's three in the afternoon.

Typically he'd be readying for a night mission, but would tell Maddox talking about home eased his mind. He'd ask crazy questions like what Maddox ate for dinner. Or he'd ask about the grapes, or ask what he planned to bottle in the coming week. He never once asked why Maddox was awake at three in the morning. At some point in the conversation, Maddox would bring up the reason he couldn't sleep.

If he could talk to Kade tonight, there would be so many questions he'd ask. He'd start by asking why he bought the property on Old Creek Road, and why he didn't tell him about it. What he wouldn't ask is where he got the money.

The other thing he'd ask is how he knew about Brodie and Peyton. Kade told him he planned to propose to Peyton when he came back from his last mission. How could he have known that their ma would ask Brodie to deliver the box of Kade's belongings to her? How could he have known that Brodie and Peyton would collide like two atoms, forming a bond so strong that even a plane crash couldn't keep them apart?

But more, how had Kade known he was ready to give Peyton up? That would be the most important question he'd ask his older brother. That's the answer he needed. How did he know? Because Maddox didn't know if he'd ever be ready to give Alex up.

Would Kade tell him to let her go, give her the chance to find a man who could love her better than he could, like Kade had told Peyton?

"I realized that I'd never love you the way you needed me to." Those were the words Kade wrote. Was that why Alex ended things with him a couple of hours short of twenty-four hours ago? Was it because Maddox could never love her the way she needed him to?

But who could love her better? Who knew Alex the way he did? No one could come close to understanding her the way he did. It wasn't just sexual either.

He understood that when Alex felt uncomfortable, she'd fly rather than fight. For years he'd let her. He didn't force her to fight for him, or for them, but there was never a time when Alex decided to come back, that he didn't open the door and invite her in.

Other women weren't one night stands, because he was never with them all night. He didn't bring them to his house. Only Alex came to his house; only Alex slept with him. He might sleep with a woman more than once, have dinner or drinks, but he never brought them around his family. If they wanted more, he'd tell them the truth. He didn't.

What would Kade have said this morning if it had been him Maddox saw in Harmony? Would he tell him to get his ass back to Alex's and tell her how he really felt? Would he tell him to admit that he thought he might love her? Or like he had with Peyton, would he tell Maddox to let her go so she could finally find someone who could love her better?

The thought of it destroyed him. The idea that he'd never hold her in his arms again made him ache. Maybe he wasn't as good a man as his older brother. Maybe he couldn't do the right thing by her and let her go, because he needed her. Had he ever told her that? How could he have when he'd just realized it himself?

He picked up his phone, thinking at first that his battery was dead. When he powered it on, it was fully charged. He didn't remember turning it off, but he must have. He'd missed a call from Gabe Avila and another from Brodie. Both had also sent texts, asking that he call as soon as he got their message. He doubted they meant three in the morning.

There was nothing from Alex, but he knew there wouldn't be.

For twenty years, they'd been playing a game. Thinking she was pregnant would have meant the end of the game, but it also would've meant the beginning of a life. Not just the baby's life, their life together. That's what he wanted, and there was only one way to find out whether something permanent would work between them.

Maybe he should start telling her how he felt, but in a way Alex could handle. He sent her a text.

If you ever wake up and think no one needs you, you're wrong. I need you, Al.

—:—

What the hell was Maddox doing? Did he sense she was serious this time, and decided to put a little effort into keeping her hooked, like a fish he reeled in and then threw back once it was caught?

Alex climbed out of bed, went into the kitchen, but couldn't decide what to do when she got there, so she went back into the bedroom. Instead of climbing into bed, knowing she wouldn't be able to go back to sleep, she picked up the clothes scattered on her floor. The things she didn't remember wearing, Alex hung back up. If she thought she might've worn it, or it was too wrinkled to wear, she threw it in the laundry hamper.

When she finished with her clothes, Alex collected shoes and put them away in the closet.

When had she last washed the sheets? Last week maybe, but since they smelled like Maddox, she pulled them off the bed and started a load of laundry.

Alex surveyed her kitchen, hands on her hips. No wonder she always went to Peyton's or ate out. Her kitchen was disgusting.

Since it was almost four, she made a pot of coffee. Doing so meant she had to wash the pot and the filter, so while she was at it, she put the rest of the dirty dishes strewn around the kitchen into the dishwasher.

By seven, her kitchen was spotless, and all but one load of laundry was done. Alex had sorted through her mail and vacuumed and dusted the living room, dining room, hallway, and bedroom. She was on her way to one of the bathrooms when she heard a car pull in the driveway.

Her reflection in the bathroom mirror looked worse than she imagined. Would Maddox care? Was it even Mad who slammed the door? Were those his footsteps coming up the walk?

Alex pulled her long hair into a tighter version of the ponytail she'd put it in three hours ago, and had just splashed cold water on her face when she heard the rap at the front door.

She took a deep breath and pulled the door open.

Her brother Enzo leaned against the door jamb, looking as though he hadn't slept in days. "Hey, Alex, can I come in?"

She nodded her head and stepped aside.

"You okay, Al?"

She wasn't. She was disappointed, but she wouldn't tell Enzo that. She'd never seen him look as shitty as he did this morning, and lately he'd been looking pretty bad.

"Am I okay? It's seven in the morning, Enzo. What are you doing here?"

He pushed past her and went into the kitchen. "Got any coffee?"

"It's old and cold. I'll make another pot."

Alex busied herself grinding the dark Columbia roast beans she preferred over Peyton's go-to French roast. All the while, she sneaked glances at her brother.

His hair wasn't gray like Gabe's and Cristobal's was, but the deep, dark circles under his eyes bothered her more than any gray hair would've.

"Enz, what's wrong?"

"Alex, I—"

She waited, watching as he sat down on the couch, leaned forward, and put his head in his hands.

"It's time for me to leave Los Cab," he began.

"Why?"

He wouldn't look at her, but she could still see the pain etched on the face he tried to hide with his hands.

"I can't do it anymore."

"Does this have something to do with Gabe coming by Stave last night?"

He shook his head. "I can't believe—"

"What? What's going on?"

"I'm in trouble, Al. So is the winery, and it's my fault."

Alex took in the words he spoke. How could the winery be in trouble? It was one of the oldest in the valley. What could Enzo have possibly done to jeopardize the family business? It had always been rock solid.

"Is this financial, Enzo?" Her question was almost a whisper.

"Worse, Al."

There was only one thing that could be worse than financial difficulties, because they could borrow money to get them through to the next harvest. "The bond?"

Without a bond, Los Cab couldn't sell the wine they made.

"Enz?"

Her brother nodded.

"What happened?"

He stood, put his hands in his pockets, and looked out the front window.

"Kade Butler."

11

Sun streamed through the double-paned bedroom window. Maddox checked his phone a dozen times, but Alex still hadn't replied to his text. Maybe she was still asleep.

She was a world-class sleeper. He'd wake up most mornings at dawn. Living a life in the vines, it was just what you did. She grew up the same way, yet Alex could easily sleep until noon.

When his phone buzzed, he saw a text from Naught, not Alex.

Get your ass out of bed.

Out.

Be ready in an hour.

Maddox turned the shower on, scrubbed his hand over his face, dropped his boxer briefs, and checked his phone one last time before getting under the stream of water.

He lost a full bedroom when he remodeled the master in order to accommodate a walk-in closet, a two-person jetted tub, and a shower big enough that if he stood in the center of it and spread his arms, he couldn't touch any of its walls.

In keeping with the design of the Scottish-style house his father built, he'd used the same rock in the shower as his home's front facade. It was open on each end, with shower heads on either side of the corridor formed by its walls. The outer wall had a two-sided, built-in panel that controlled the shower and the tub.

His favorite part was the hundreds of tiny streams of water that flowed from the rectangular-shaped unit set into the ceiling. When it was on, it felt as though he was standing under a waterfall.

How many times had he pushed Alex up against this wall of stone? It looked hard and cold, but it was filled with radiant heat.

He'd press her body against it, lift her and spread her legs over his, and take her from behind. He'd reach over to the control panel and fill the tub, and then, keeping their bodies joined, he'd ease her into the warm, jetting water.

The tile floor had drains built into the stone in several places, so it wouldn't matter if they spilled all the water from the tub as he slammed his body into hers again and again.

He rested his head against the stone, wishing she were with him now, and not just because his body craved hers.

He and Naughton were spending the day working at the property on Old Creek Road. Every minute he was there, he longed to show her all the secrets he'd discovered.

There was at least one more he hadn't found yet, and Naughton insisted it was better than all the others they'd seen thus far. He almost didn't want to find it until he could be certain Alex would be with him when he did.

—:—

"I don't understand what Kade could have to do with Los Cab's bond, Enzo. He never worked in the industry, and even if he had, why would he or anyone else report us?"

"I wish I could tell you more, Alex. But I can't. If I do, it'll make you as liable as I am. I just came by to tell you I'm leaving." Enzo leaned forward and kissed her cheek.

Alex wrapped her arms around his waist and held tight. "Don't go. Whatever has happened, we can work it out as a family."

"This is all on me, Alex. It isn't fair that the rest of you pay the price for what I did."

"But won't we have to if you disappear?"

"I'm not disappearing."

Alex's phone was vibrating on the kitchen counter. When she saw it was Peyton, she turned to pick it up.

"I need to get this, Enz, but I'll just be a minute."

When Alex turned back around, her brother was gone. She ran outside, but was too late to catch him before he drove away. Peyton's call went to voicemail, but Alex called her right back.

"Hey, Peyton. Sorry, I was just talking to Enzo—"

"Alex! He's done it."

"Who?" Alex could barely understand Peyton, she was talking so fast, and crying at the same time.

"Lang!"

"Okay, okay. Slow down. What has he done?"

"Here. Talk to Brodie." Alex heard the phone jostle.

"Hey, Alex. Sorry to call so early, but Peyton's pretty upset."

She looked over at the clock. She'd been awake so long it felt more like noon than seven thirty. "What has Lang done now?"

"He's managed to get the custody hearing moved back up."

"When is it?"

"Later this week. Listen, is there any chance you could come over? Peyton is—"

"I'll be right there."

Alex looked in the bathroom mirror one last time before she walked out the door. She'd changed her clothes and tightened her ponytail again, but she still looked like crap. What would they expect, though, at this hour of the morning?

Her stomach rumbled when she got in the car, reminding her she'd finished almost an entire pot of coffee on her own and hadn't eaten anything. She'd need food if she was going to be of any help to Peyton.

Stopping for food. She texted.

Thanks. Peyton answered.

Damn that Lang Becker. What would compel him to file a petition for custody of Peyton's boys anyway? It didn't make any sense. He'd left Peyton and the boys seven years ago, saying he'd realized having kids really wasn't his "thing," and he was moving in with a woman who didn't have any.

Lang hadn't been great about paying child support either, until not long after Peyton started seeing Kade. She couldn't confirm it, but Peyton told Alex she had a feeling Kade had paid Lang a visit and *convinced* him he should support his sons.

Peyton found out about the petition three weeks ago, and the Wolfs' family attorney got it pushed out six weeks, citing Peyton was on bed rest and wouldn't be able to attend the hearing. Somehow Lang got it moved up. Maybe he found out Peyton was no longer on bed rest and convinced the judge to act.

Alex stopped on Moonstone Beach Road at the Ollalieberry Diner. Peyton's favorite, ollalieberry and cream cheese muffins, would still be warm this early in the morning. She picked up several, for the boys and Brodie too, and then added a half-dozen peach and cream that she could take home later. They were her favorite. Not just hers, Mad's too.

Why did everything in her life have to remind her of Maddox? She still hadn't figured out how to respond to the weird text he'd sent in the middle of the night. Had he somehow known she was awake?

Alex pulled into the driveway and saw Jamison sitting on the bench in the front yard. She got out of the car and walked over to him instead of going inside.

"Can I join you?"

He didn't answer but scooted over to give her room on the bench. She held the bag of muffins open.

"Hungry?"

Jamison shrugged, but then reached his hand inside the bag. Warm ollalieberry muffins were hard for anyone to resist.

"How come you're sittin' out here?"

"Mom's upset about something, but she and Brodie are trying to stay real quiet about whatever it is."

"Why do you think she's upset?"

He shrugged his shoulders. "Maybe something's wrong with my baby sister. Mom is trying to pretend like she's not crying, but I know she is."

"It's not your baby sister. She's fine. Your mom is upset, though."

Jamison nodded.

"I've known your mom almost her whole life. We started hanging out together when we were about your age."

"I know." Jamison smiled. He'd probably heard stories of Peyton and Alex his entire childhood.

"So, here's what I know more than anything else. Your mom doesn't hide things from you. She may not tell you what's upsetting her right away, because she's too sad or mad or whatever she's feeling. But she does tell you. Right, kiddo?"

"Yeah, I guess."

"Try to be patient, and know that, as soon as she's ready, she'll tell you. In the meantime, go get Finn and take him down to the beach. I was there yesterday, and there are tons of moonstones."

"Can I have another muffin first?"

Alex messed up his hair. "Yep. Good thing I bought a bunch of 'em, huh?"

Jamison walked up to the house, and Alex followed. "Take one for your brother too."

"Okay. Thanks, Aunt Alex."

"Come here." She put her hand on Jamison's shoulder and pulled him into a hug. "You're not getting too big to hug me yet, are ya?"

He smiled and shook his head before going down the hallway to get his brother.

"Thank you." Peyton stood and hugged Alex too. "For the muffins and for talking to Jamie."

"He thought it was something with the baby. I didn't tell him why you're upset, but I did tell him his baby sister is fine." Alex glanced at Peyton's ever-expanding tummy and felt the familiar, empty ache in her own.

"Thanks for coming over." Brodie hugged her like Jamie and Peyton had. "And for the muffins."

"You're welcome, but you better eat quick. Jamie's had two and took another for Finn."

Brodie offered the bag to Peyton first, but she shook her head. "I can't eat right now."

Alex watched as he put the bag on the kitchen counter and rested his hand on Peyton's belly. "She needs to eat, sweetheart."

Alex's eyes filled with tears, and she turned away. "Be right back," she murmured, already on her way to the guest bathroom.

Splashing cold water on her face was turning into a habit. This was the third time she'd done it this morning. She looked in the mirror, wishing the water would get rid of the bags under her eyes.

It was hard enough now for her to be around Peyton and Brodie. How would it be once the baby was born?

Especially knowing Maddox wasn't in her life, and wouldn't be again. Peyton was intuitive and knew Alex as well as Alex knew her. She had a lot on her mind right now, so she might not be as aware of Alex's moods or emotions, but soon she would be, and then she'd want to talk about it.

"Bye," she heard Jamie shout from the other side of the door.

"Bye," she shouted back. "See you later."

"Thanks for the muffins, Aunt Alex," Finn shouted.

"You're welcome, sweetheart."

This was silly. She was shouting at her godsons through the bathroom door so they wouldn't know she was crying too, although for a reason completely different than their mother's.

She took a deep breath and walked back into the kitchen. "Okay, tell me about the hearing," she began.

"It's on Friday," said Brodie.

"This Friday?"

Both Brodie and Peyton nodded their heads.

"What did Stan say?" Stan had been the Wolf family attorney for years. He'd also known most of the lawyers and judges in the valley longer than Alex and Peyton had been alive.

"He's optimistic, although he believes Lang must have a good reason to believe he will prevail. Otherwise, he wouldn't be so anxious for the hearing," Brodie answered.

"This makes no sense. Why wouldn't he just ask to see them? Why petition for custody?"

"Do you mind if I tell her?" Brodie asked Peyton.

"Of course not."

"From what Peyton's father told me, Lang is getting married again. Stan believes the new wife's family disapproves of Lang's lack of a relationship with Jamison and Finn."

"So? That doesn't sound like a good reason to allow him to file this petition."

"The judge who signed the petition is Lang's future wife's uncle."

"Shit."

"Right."

"How can he do this? Those boys don't even know him," cried Peyton. "He expects them to want to live at his house half their life?"

Alex didn't want to make Peyton feel worse, but the fact that the new wife's uncle was the judge hearing the petition, filled her with dread. Why hadn't Stan suggested he recuse himself? There wasn't any way he could be impartial.

"Maddox and Naughton are on their way here now. Between the five of us, I'm hoping we can figure out what our strategy will be on Friday."

"Why? I mean what do Mad or Naught know about custody hearings? Shouldn't you be strategizing with your lawyer, Peyton?"

Dammit, Maddox was on his way here. What could she do? Leave?

"Stan's on his way, too. So are Jamison and August."

Maybe with her parents, her lawyer, Brodie and his brothers there, Peyton wouldn't mind if she left.

Of course she'd mind. Peyton needed her there as much as anyone else. Alex had stood beside her friend when she married Lang, and then when she divorced him. She'd also stood by her when Kade died, and then again when they believed Brodie died in a plane crash. Alex couldn't leave now, just because being around Maddox made her uncomfortable. There'd been plenty of other times they'd been forced to be in the same room when they couldn't stand the sight of each other. This would be no different.

"Hey, Alex, did you find out why Gabe was looking for Mad and Naught last night?" Brodie asked.

"Uh, no. Not really." It must've had something to do with the bond issues Enzo had alluded to this morning. But he said they were in trouble because of Kade. Until Alex knew more, she wasn't about to discuss it in front of Peyton.

Alex walked over to the front window, wishing Maddox weren't on his way here. She might as well get used to seeing him, since Peyton was her best friend and Brodie was his brother. She'd probably have to see Maddox at family gatherings for the rest of her life. And what about the wedding? Peyton would definitely ask her to be her maid of honor again, and Brodie would surely want Maddox to stand up for him. Maybe Alex would be able to talk them into eloping.

"I wonder where they are. They left the ranch over an hour ago," said Brodie, looking at his phone.

Alex had been wondering the same thing. She'd eaten all but two of the peach muffins, knowing Mad would want more than one. Why she was saving them for him was beyond her, but she was.

Another fifteen minutes passed before they heard Mad's truck pull into the driveway. Alex had almost worn the carpet through near the front window, pacing back and forth.

Naughton came through the door first, followed by Mad, who looked over at her before anyone else.

"What took you so long?" Brodie asked.

Maddox broke his gaze from hers and looked at Naughton.

"You tell them," Naughton said.

"The hearing has been postponed indefinitely, pending dismissal of the request."

"What did you do?" Alex blurted.

"I took care of it," Maddox snapped at her.

Alex sat next to Peyton, who still hadn't gotten any color back in her cheeks.

"He said Naught and I weren't the first Butlers to visit him, though."

"Who else had?" Peyton asked.

"We don't know," answered Naught.

Maddox was staring at her as though he was trying to tell her something with his eyes.

"I stopped at the diner and got muffins. They're probably cold now, but here they are." Alex walked over to Naughton first and held the plate out to him. He started to take a peach muffin, and then smirked at Mad before taking the last ollalieberry.

She walked over to Maddox and handed the plate to him. "What's going on?" she whispered.

"You wouldn't believe it if I told you," he answered, just as quietly.

"Walk?"

"Definitely."

—:—

Alex was going to think he'd lost his mind, but he had to tell someone what Lang had told him and Naughton, and he wasn't about to tell Brodie or Peyton.

"What happened, Mad?" Alex asked, catching up to him.

He was halfway down the street, headed toward Moonstone Beach.

"Walk with me, Alex."

"Walk? How about run? Can you slow down, please?"

"Sorry." He doubted he could slow down. Nervous energy was eating him up. More than anything, he was close to believing he was losing his mind.

"Maddox?" Alex stopped in the middle of the street. He turned around and saw she had her hands on her hips, and she was breathing harder than she should be.

"Shit, Alex. I'm sorry. Your surgery." He walked back to where she was and took her hand. "I'll go slower."

"What's got you all fired up?"

Her. But that wasn't all. He wanted to get to the beach before he told her what Lang said and what had happened yesterday after he left her house. "I'll tell you in a minute." He needed to sit and take a few deep breaths of ocean air.

"Okay, mister mysterious." She squeezed his hand.

It was crowded at the beach, at least up on the boardwalk. Maddox forgot today was Sunday and tourists would be milling about.

It was almost fifty steps down to the sand from where they stood. "You okay walking down?"

She nodded and walked ahead of him. When they got near the water, Alex sat on the sand.

"We're here. Start talking."

"You sure you're okay, Al? Your breathing…"

"I'm fine, for now." She turned around and looked at the steps that led back up to the boardwalk. "You may have to carry me back up, though."

"Not a problem," he murmured. "Come here." He had to feel her body next to his. With the rest of the shit swirling around in his head, he needed the constant in his life that was Alex. She let him pull her close, and rested her head on his shoulder. When he fell back on the sand, she came with him and put her head on his chest.

"Remember when Peyton thought she saw Kade? After my ma's heart attack?"

"Yeah."

"The same thing happened when I left your house yesterday morning. Except Kade didn't talk to me."

"What do you mean?"

"I thought I saw him. I mean, I could've sworn I saw him."

Maddox told her how he'd stopped in Harmony to get some breakfast, and about the man he'd seen walking across the street.

"It was probably just someone who looked like him."

"That's what I thought too. But then, when we stopped to talk to Lang this morning…"

"What?"

"He said our brother had been to see him." Maddox sat back up, gently bringing Alex with him. "It didn't make sense to Naught and me, since Brodie had just called and asked us to come over. Why would he if he'd already talked to Lang?"

"Why did he?"

"He didn't. That's the thing. Naughton asked him when he'd talked to Brodie. Shit, I can't even say this out loud."

"What? *Jesus.* Tell me."

"He said Kade came to see him."

Alex looked as pale as he'd expected her to.

"Did he say anything else?"

"No, but it was obvious that whoever else paid him a visit left him shaken."

"You think someone told Lang he was Kade."

"What other explanation could there be?"

"But?"

"After we left Lang's, Naught told me Kade had talked to Peyton's ex-husband once before."

"We thought he had. About child support?"

"Yep."

"You think Lang would've recognized him?"

"You got it."

"No offense to Kade, Maddox, but those guys do all look kind of alike, especially with their shaved heads and muscle-bound bodies."

"You're right." He'd thought of that too. It was the only explanation he could come up with. Kade must've enlisted one of the guys he used to work with to keep an eye on Peyton, and maybe on their entire family.

"Whoever it is, would want to stay under the radar."

"Right about that too." Telling Alex was the best thing he could've done. She helped him see there was a logical explanation when he couldn't come up with one on his own. "Thanks, Al."

"Anytime, Mad."

"So tell me what you did to Lang."

"I'll let your imagination run wild instead."

"Yeah? Did you beat him up, Mad? Did you break his nose? What about his fingers?"

Maddox laughed. "None of the above."

"How'd you get him to back off, then?"

"You aren't the only one who knows what happens in this valley, Alex."

"You have something on him."

Maddox shrugged but smiled.

They stayed silent for maybe ten or fifteen min-utes, long enough that Maddox couldn't keep quiet any longer.

"You didn't answer my text."

Alex brought her knees up to her chest and wrapped her arms around them. "Did it need an answer?"

What the hell? If she sent him a text saying she needed him, he damn well would've answered her.

"I guess you didn't think so."

"We're friends. We'll be friends until we're old and I'm gray," she grinned. "How come you don't have gray hair? Or do you color it like Kade did?"

"What are you talking about?"

"Kade colored his goatee."

"How do you know?"

"I saw him at one of those warehouse beauty supply places in San Luis Obispo. I walked up and asked if he thought Peyton would look better as a brunette."

Maddox laughed. "What did he say?"

"You know how Kade was. He straight out told me why he was buying hair dye. Pointed to the guy on the box too, just so I knew he wouldn't buy ladies' shit."

Maddox closed his eyes and concentrated on the feel of the breeze on his face. He looked out at the ocean. The sea went on and on and on. There was no end to it. Wherever it banked was thousands of miles from here, and whoever watched the same water he watched had no idea he existed. He was inconsequential to most of the world, but here, he wanted someone to need him. Not someone. *Alex.*

"Last night I should've asked if you needed me too, Alex."

12

Of course she did, far more than she'd admit to him. She always would, but that didn't matter. What mattered was that Maddox could never be the man she needed him to be.

"I told you, Mad. We're friends. We always will be. I just think we've reached the age where we have to stop using each other for sex."

"Why?"

She laughed. "It's time we both let each other go, so we can get out there and find the great loves of our lives, get married, make babies, and live happily ever after. Just like Brodie and Peyton."

"Is that what you want, Alex?"

"It is, and I can't have that if I'm always falling back on you."

"That's how you see it?"

"That's how it is. It always has been. I don't have to put myself out there, because when I'm feeling lonely, I run back to you. You scratch my itches, and you make me feel all sexy. It can't always be you, Mad. Someday I have to find someone who isn't you."

"You think I should find someone else too?"

"Yes, Maddox. Look at us. We're in our thirties. You're almost *forty,* for Christ's sake. We've had the same relationship for twenty years. One of us has to be mature enough to say it's time we both move on. I've been waiting on you to be the mature one, but at this point, I guess it's all on me."

Alex smiled, tried to joke with him, but inside she was dying. He hadn't said he wanted to be the man she was looking for. He hadn't said he wanted to be her great love, to marry her, and have babies with her. He hadn't said anything.

"You can give this up, Al?" Maddox leaned over and ran his tongue up the side of her neck. "What about this, baby?" He put his hand under her shirt and squeezed her breast through her bra. His fingers played with her hardened nipple while his tongue continued to torment her. He brought his hand back out from under her shirt and gripped her chin. "What about this, Alex?" He covered her mouth with his, and when she opened to him, his tongue did battle with hers. He brought her with him when he rested back on the sand, and rolled so she was on top of him.

"You feel me, Alex?"

She squeezed her eyes tight, willing the tears to stay inside where they belonged. When she knew they wouldn't, she pushed off of him. "Stop it. This is what I'm talking about, Maddox."

She took off in the direction of the steps, knowing that by the time she reached the top, she'd need to sit and rest before she walked home. It didn't matter; she had to get away from him before she did what she always did, and fell right back into bed with him.

She gripped the wooden rail and willed her body to give her the strength to make it to the top of the stairs, and then the strength not to succumb to the way Maddox Butler made her feel.

On the fifth step, she felt him behind her. Maddox swept her up and carried her to the top as though she didn't weigh an ounce. Being in his arms, feeling his strength, was everything she wanted in life. But she also wanted his heart. Without it, she'd never be happy, and if she wasn't happy, she'd make Maddox miserable.

—:—

They walked back to the house without speaking. Maddox would've, if he could've figured out what to say. But what was there? Alex had told him she wanted to find the great love of her life. That had to mean it wasn't him. He knew that, or should have, considering she'd never told him she loved him.

He was her itch-scratcher. The guy who made Alex feel good. Was that how it had always been?

Instead of feeling boxed in, unable to fight, as he'd always believed, the reality was she used him when she was lonely. All these years, he thought he had her number, but, boy, was he wrong. He didn't know Alex Avila at all. What a schmuck.

No more, though. He could move on too. There were plenty of women who thought he was happily ever after material. Plenty. But he'd always held back for Alex. Alex was the only woman who slept in his bed. Alex was the only woman who parked in his barn. Alex was the only woman as comfortable in his house as he was. It had never been what he believed it to be though.

That's why she said no when he asked her to move in with him. It wasn't because she was scared; it was because she didn't want to.

"Maddox—"

"Don't, Alex. I get it, okay? Time to move on. You're convenient, and so am I."

Maddox walked ahead of her, relieved to see Naughton in the driveway. "You ready to go?"

"Yeah. Everything okay?"

"Never better," he answered, just as Alex walked past him. "Right, Al?"

She didn't answer, didn't even look at him. If things were the way they had been even a month ago, she would've flipped him off at least.

"What was that?" Naught asked.

"Nothing."

"Bullshit."

"What do you want me to tell you, Naught? You wanna hear how Alex Avila just crapped all over me?"

Naught shook his head. "You do it to each other."

"Not anymore."

They drove to the vineyard on Old Creek Road in silence, the same way he and Alex had walked back to Peyton's house. Maddox had nothing to say, and Naughton—he *never* had anything to say.

—:—

Peyton was waiting for her when she came back inside. "Alex?"

"Yeah?"

"Are you okay?"

"Nope."

"Wanna talk about it?"

Alex turned around from where she stood near the front window. Brodie was nowhere in sight.

"Brodie left," Peyton explained. "He drove down to the beach, picked up the boys, and took them back to his parents' place so they can ride this afternoon."

Of course he did. Because Brodie was the perfect f'ing guy. It wasn't Peyton's fault, but there was no way Alex could be around her right now. Peyton had everything Alex wanted in life, and being with her just made Alex's heart hurt more.

"I gotta go. I'm really glad everything worked out with Lang. I would've hated to see him get a minute with those sweet boys."

"I don't know. Maybe—"

"I'll see ya, Peyton," Alex said before Peyton could continue. "I'll call you later."

"Wait." Peyton came out the door Alex had just left through. "Where are you going?"

"Home. I gotta get some rest." Alex was in her car and out the driveway before Peyton could say anything else.

Enough with worrying about other people. It was time Alex focused on herself and her family.

Enzo had left this morning without telling her where he was going. Gabe wasn't returning her phone calls, and neither was Trev. If what Enzo told her this morning was true, their family's winery, their heritage, was in jeopardy, and somehow, it was Kade Butler's fault. He was keeping pretty busy for a dead guy.

Instead of going home, Alex drove to Los Caballeros. She intended to get to the bottom of whatever the hell was going on with their bond, and see if she could get it fixed before they lost everything.

—:—

"Where do you want to start?" Maddox asked.

"At the top." Naughton showed Maddox a rough outline of how he envisioned utilizing the four hundred acres they owned between them. Thirty acres would be set aside for Maddox to have a barn with stables for horses if he wanted them.

By Naught's estimations, it would take three to five years before the first vineyards they planted would yield enough fruit for adequate production. By year six or seven, he believed the majority of their workable land would be fully planted with fruit-producing vines.

"Most of the other two hundred hectares are plantable, according to Lena."

The first five years would be tough, but once they reached full production, a conservative net income estimate was between two and three million a year, just from the four hundred acres they had now.

Owning their land outright gave them plenty of collateral to finance the initial phases of Naughton's plan. Their production would be twice that of Butler Ranch. If they added the other two hundred hectares, it would be almost four times as much.

Instead of purchasing the remaining land at this time, Maddox would propose Lena give them first right of refusal.

Taking on another winery operation would require a significant amount of time and money. To get things underway, they'd need a large labor force to get the vineyards into production as quickly as possible.

"You done overthinking everything yet?" asked Naughton. "If you are, let's get to work."

They were headed back to Maddox's truck when Lena approached.

"You two have been head-to-head out in this heat for over an hour. Can I get you something to drink?"

"You been watchin' us, Lena?" Maddox winked. If he was going to move on from Alex Avila, he would take advantage of flirting whenever he was in the presence of a woman who appealed to him. While she definitely wasn't his type, Lena Hess was an extraordinarily attractive woman and was probably just as lonely as he was going to be.

"I can see everything, Maddox. Best not to forget that."

"You say you can see everything. Do you know anything about the wine barrels stored in the caves?"

Lena shook her head, but there was something in the way she blinked several times in rapid succession and her eyes darted back and forth, that led Maddox to believe she knew something she didn't want him to know she knew.

"How about that drink?" Naughton said to Lena, who appeared stunned by Maddox's question.

"Of course. What would you like? Lemonade, water, or something stronger?"

Maddox definitely wanted something stronger, but now wasn't a good time for it. He and Naughton had a lot of work to do, and for that, he'd need his wits about him. As hot as it was going to be today, alcohol would go straight to his head.

"Water's good. Thanks."

"Naughton?"

"Same."

Lena went inside, but neither he nor Naught followed.

"She knows something," Naught murmured.

"Damn right, she does."

"She's protecting somebody. Who do you think it is, Mad?"

"No idea."

"I was hoping she'd tell us where the barrels came from, and there wouldn't be anything sinister behind it."

"Me too, brother."

If this land didn't mean the fulfillment of his dreams as a winemaker, Maddox might consider walking away from it. In the days since he'd found out about it, things, both in his life and with this property, kept getting weirder and weirder. Maybe the land was cursed.

—:—

Alex sat in her mother's kitchen, not knowing what to do next. She'd expected to find Gabe here, working in the vineyards or the winery, but the field manager said he hadn't been there since Friday. It wasn't unusual for him to take the weekend off, especially at this time of the year, but if they were in trouble, why would he stay away? They all needed to come together and fix whatever was wrong.

Enzo wasn't here, not that she'd expected him to be, but Alex certainly expected to see Trev, who wasn't here either.

Her mother showed no sign of worry or concern, which put Alex in a difficult position. Did she ask her mother if she was aware of any issues?

"Mama, where is everyone?"

"I don't know, *mija.* Who are you looking for?"

"Gabe, Enzo, Trev."

"Have you tried calling them?"

Alex nodded, deciding she wouldn't say more. She wished she'd remembered to ask Maddox this morning if he'd talked to Gabe, but with everything else going on, she forgot.

Obviously he hadn't, or Maddox would've said something to her. Or would he? He hadn't told her about the Old Creek Road property, and that had to be the biggest thing that had ever happened to him.

Her mother stood behind her and ran her fingers through Alex's hair. "What's troubling you, *mija*?"

"Everything is changing."

"That's life, isn't it?"

"I'm thirty-two years old, and nothing has changed in my life other than Papa dying. Now, all of a sudden, *everything* is different."

"Everything?"

"Peyton, Brodie, Maddox, Gabe, Enzo, even Kade."

"What has changed with your brothers?"

Alex shrugged. "They aren't here."

"They don't live here, *mija*. They haven't for a long time. Why don't you tell me what's really going on?"

"I thought I was pregnant." Alex put her face in her hands and cried. "I wanted to be pregnant, Mama."

Her mother was at least six inches shorter than Alex, but she sat and pulled her onto her lap anyway, rocking her back and forth.

"Shh, *mija*," she murmured again and again.

When Alex stopped crying, she moved back over to the chair she'd been sitting in.

"How does Maddox feel about you not being pregnant?"

Alex was stunned that her mother would ask, but she really shouldn't have been. The woman had seven children. She probably saw a lot more than she acknowledged to any of them.

"I'm not sure. When I thought I was, he said he was happy. Those weren't his exact words, but he said he wanted the baby."

"And when you told him you weren't?"

"He didn't really say. I guess he was disappointed, but I wonder if he was really more relieved."

"I doubt that."

"Why? What do you see that I don't?"

"Maddox loves you, Alex. He has for years."

"No, Mama, you're wrong. Maddox has never loved me."

"No less than you love him."

"Do I? I told Papa I did. I went to Moonstone Beach yesterday and let the sand run through my fingers. I told him I wished he'd known Maddox, and what a good man he is. Maddox saved us after Papa died, and I just wish…" She couldn't continue, she was crying too hard.

"He knew, *mija*."

"I know you believe Papa looks down on us, but I wish he *really* knew, Mama."

"He knew you were in love with Maddox."

"What?"

"Do you think your Papa and I are blind?"

"Why didn't you ever say anything? Why didn't Papa?"

"I told you, Alex. Your father knew Maddox was a good man."

"Why didn't he…"

"Make amends with Laird Butler?"

Alex nodded.

"You tell me how it would've gone. Tell me the story of your papa and Laird Butler setting aside their differences and becoming friends."

It never could've happened. Her father was too proud, and so was Laird. Neither would've extended the olive branch. Even if Maddox found a way to bring the two families together, Alex doubted that anything short of a disaster in both their vineyards could have bridged the gap between the two men.

"There he is," her mother said, looking out the window.

"Who?"

"Gabriel."

Alex ran out the back door, slamming it behind her.

"¡Por Dios!" she heard her mother shout.

Gabe got out of his truck but didn't look at her. "Alex."

"What's going on, Gabe? Where's Enzo, and why did you come looking for Maddox last night?"

"Did Enzo come see you?"

"He did, and he told me we're in trouble. How bad is it?"

"Follow me," he barked.

13

Maddox and Naughton spent hours roaming the Old Creek Road property, discussing their options, estimating costs, determining which of the vineyards Naughton would try to save, and which they'd replant.

If Maddox had to guess, he'd say they walked ten miles today, easily. A lot, given four hundred acres was only a little over half a square mile. Even then, there was land they hadn't covered and something significant he hadn't found yet.

He and Naughton agreed that the northernmost one-hundred-acre vineyards, which also sat at the highest elevation, would be dedicated to various Pinot Noir clones, as well as Sauvignon Blanc.

Moving southwest on the property, the next vineyards would be planted with Cabernet Sauvignon, Cabernet Franc, Merlot, and Syrah.

Farthest south, and also at the lowest elevation, they'd plant Chardonnay and Zinfandel.

Smaller vineyards scattered around the property would be dedicated to Petit Verdot, Grenache, and Carignan, as well as Roussanne and Viognier.

Maddox was equally exhausted physically and mentally, yet throughout the day, his mind drifted back to his conversation with Alex.

Roaming the land at Butler Ranch always gave him clarity and a sense of peace. It was no different walking this land.

Thinking Alex was pregnant did a number on him. Maddox began envisioning things he'd never considered. The same had to be true for her. Maybe that was where the "find the love of her life" stuff was coming from.

She had been through a lot in the last two weeks. She'd helped Peyton and Brodie get back together, thought she was pregnant, found out she wasn't, and had major surgery. She also said that Cris told her it would take some time for the effects of the anesthesia to wear off.

He'd give her some space. It wasn't as though either one of them were going to fall in love and marry someone else tomorrow.

"Where'd you go?" Naught asked.

"What do you mean? I'm right here."

"I asked you the same question three times."

"Sorry. What did you ask me?"

"What are you going to do about Alex Avila?"

—:—

"This is crazy." Alex shook her head. "Where is Enzo now?"

"He went to see Trev, who convinced him he was panicking over nothing."

"Why the urgency to talk to Maddox Butler, then?"

"That doesn't concern you."

"Seriously, Gabe? I've been trying to reach all three of you since last night. You couldn't call me back and tell me there was nothing to worry about?"

"You're as bad as Enzo."

Alex was furious that she'd spent the whole day worrying that their family was on the brink of bankruptcy, and Enzo was on his way to jail, yet Gabe had the nerve to tell her she was overreacting.

"You're a jerk. You don't take me or Enzo seriously."

"Tell you what, *princess,* you start behaving like someone who should be taken seriously, and I'll start doing it."

"What's that supposed to mean?"

"You've been chasing after Maddox Butler since you were a teenager. Don't you have any pride, Alex? You're nothing more than his—"

Before he said something she couldn't unhear, Alex slapped Gabe across the face as hard as she could. *"How dare you!"*

The side of Gabe's face was red with her handprint. "Truth hurts you worse than that slap hurt me. If Papa were still alive—"

"You're wrong, Gabe. You're wrong about Maddox. How could you, after all he did for our family?"

Gabe shook his head and walked toward the winery. Alex was too stunned to move. Was that really the way he saw her? Was he the only one, or did Enzo and Trev think the same thing? What about Cristobal? Surely he didn't share Gabe's opinion.

"Alex," her mother called out to her from the back door, waving her cell phone. "Someone is trying to reach you."

There wasn't anyone she could think of that she wanted to talk to, but she walked back to the house anyway.

What was she saying to her mother before Gabe drove up? Everything was changing, and none of it in a good way. Maybe it was time Alex made some drastic changes of her own, beginning with getting away from this place for a while.

—:—

"Nothing. There isn't anything to do."

Naughton shrugged and opened the passenger door of the truck. "We made a lot of progress today."

"We will tomorrow, too."

Tomorrow, Naughton would call the labor contractor and hire the workforce they'd need to begin transforming the vineyards.

"We should look for a field manager now, so he knows the vineyards from the beginning," Naught suggested.

"Good idea. I'll let you handle the hiring process. Since we're in the slowest time of the year, I'll start looking for an apprentice winery manager too."

"That's on you."

"I'll get a few candidates in line, and then we can make the final decision on both together."

Naughton shrugged again. Hiring people wasn't his favorite thing to do. Worse, was getting to know them once they were hired. If there was a part of Naught's job he could eliminate, it would be training new staff.

Maddox didn't mind handling the interviews, but in the case of the field manager, Naughton knew what to look for better than he did.

Maddox was just about to put the truck in gear and leave when he saw Lena walking toward them, waving. Naught rolled the passenger door window down.

"What do you need?" he asked.

"Nice," Maddox mumbled.

"What?"

Lena walked around to Maddox's side of the truck rather than to Naught's open window.

"Can we talk?"

Obviously, she didn't mean now. Did she? "Of course. I'll be back tomorrow morning. Name the time."

"No, tonight."

Maddox guessed Lena didn't want to talk to both him and Naughton, since she came to his side of the truck.

"We can meet after I take Naught back to the ranch."

"Let's meet in Paso Robles."

"Got a place in mind?"

"Il Conti, in an hour."

Il Conti was a swanky Italian place just off the main square. He'd need a little more time to get cleaned up if that's where she wanted to go.

"Give me an hour and a half."

Lena nodded and walked away from the truck. She wasn't the happiest person Maddox ever met, but that was understandable. Her mother had died, who knew where her father was, and she hadn't mentioned any other family. Maddox couldn't imagine being so alone in the world.

"Hornet's nest there," Naughton commented.

"What's worse than hornets?"

Naught laughed.

—:—

Rory Calder called three times before Alex decided he must have an important reason for being so persistent, and answered.

"Hey, Rory."

"Alex, I'm glad I reached you finally."

"Uh, yeah, about that? What's so urgent?"

"I'm headed back up north tomorrow and was wondering if we could get together tonight?"

She was about to ask why, but then decided if she was really going to move on from Maddox, she needed to say yes more than she said no. She wasn't all that interested in Rory, but practice dating wouldn't hurt.

"Sure, that would be great. Do you want to meet at Stave?"

"I was thinking somewhere farther inland. Where are you now?"

"At Los Cab, do you—"

"Great, I'll pick you up in forty-five minutes. Il Conti good?"

"Uh, okay." He was as pushy as he was persistent.

What the hell was she going to wear? She didn't have time to drive back to Cambria, change her clothes, and be back here before Rory arrived. Instead, she texted him.

Just remembered I have another meeting in town. Meet you at 6:30.

A meeting on a Sunday? Oh well, shopping qualified as a meeting, didn't it?

She'd rather have her own car, anyway. There was something about Rory that bugged her. If whatever he wanted to talk to her about got weird, she could leave.

Alex, Alex, his response said. What was that supposed to mean?

There was a sweet little boutique in town that would have everything she needed, even some sexy lingerie. Not that she needed sexy lingerie tonight, but soon she would, and she wouldn't want to wear anything with her "new man" that Maddox had already seen her in.

If she was quick, she'd have time for a quick glass of wine to settle her nerves before she met Rory. It had been one hell of a day. The worst part of it was her conversation with Gabe. Followed closely by her conversation with Maddox.

Gabe had told her Los Caballeros did have some potential problems with their bond, that as their compliance manager, Enzo should've caught. If he got on top of it, they might face some penalties, but it wouldn't be a substantial amount, and they certainly wouldn't lose their bond altogether.

There was more to it than Gabe was telling her, and since he made it clear he didn't respect her opinion, it was unlikely he'd be straight with her.

Her oldest brother never gave her much credit, but when she was on her game, there wasn't anything that happened in the Central Coast wine industry she didn't know about. If he or her other brothers were hiding something, she'd find out what it was all on her own.

Il Conti was quiet for a Sunday night. Rather than checking in with the hostess, Alex sat at the bar to wait for Rory.

"Hey, Alex," the bartender greeted her.

"Hey, Jimmy. I didn't know you worked here."

"Here, there, and everywhere these days. Trying to get out of the service industry and into my own wine operation."

"Do you have land?"

"Nah, that's part of working myself to death, so I can pick up a few acres and at least get started."

Jimmy had been winemaker for several small wineries, primarily on the eastside. Alex would've thought he'd make more money doing that than tending bar.

"Where else are you working?"

He named a couple of other restaurants in town, but no wineries. Something was up with that, too.

"You're lookin' smokin' hot tonight, by the way. Special occasion?"

Alex smiled. "Thanks, Jimmy, furthest thing from it. Just decided a new dress and pair of shoes might brighten my day."

She'd picked out a pale peach sleeveless sheath and nude pumps with three-inch heels. From what she remembered, Rory wasn't that much taller than she was. Having a little height on him might discourage him from getting too grabby.

"You sure brightened my day, sweetheart."

Alex smiled when Jimmy winked, but he wasn't dating material either. It didn't make sense that he wasn't making wine anymore, and if he was looking for an investor by way of a girlfriend to help him get his land, she wasn't an option.

"You're early." Rory came up behind her, leaned forward, and kissed her cheek. "Hi, Alex."

Alex leaned away. "Hi, Rory. You're early too." And a little familiar for someone she didn't know very well.

"What are you drinking?"

"It's a Pear Valley Charbono. Have you tried it?"

"I'm not big on cult wines."

Alex would've rolled her eyes if Rory weren't looking right at her. Charbono was hardly a cult wine. It was produced in small amounts, and somewhat scarce, because it was so damn good, not because it was a fad.

The grape had a shared Italian and French heritage, given it was originally grown in the Piedmont and

Savoie regions. The direct translation for its official name, Douce Noir, was "sweet black," and while the wine had no residual sugar whatsoever, it was inky black in color.

"Let's move to a table, shall we?" Alex was ready to get this dinner over with as quickly as possible, not only to get away from Rory, but also because the longer she was around people in the wine industry, the more she realized she needed a break.

Rory motioned for her to sit in the two-top's chair while he sat on the bench side facing the entrance. Two things about that bugged Alex. First, he didn't make any attempt to get her chair, and second, it was rude not to ask which she'd prefer. She hated sitting with her back to the door.

"So, Rory. What can I do for you?"

The waiter, someone else Alex knew in the valley, arrived to take their order, and just to irritate Rory, Alex suggested they order a bottle of the Charbono.

"I think I'll stick with something more my style, but by all means, please, order another glass."

"Would you like to hear tonight's specials?" the waiter asked.

"I'm ready," Rory said before Alex had a chance to respond.

"Of course we would." She knew what she planned to order, but Rory was irritating the crap out of her.

Once they were ready to order, he went first. What a surprise.

Alex asked again what she could do for him.

"I wanted to have dinner with a beautiful woman. Does there need to be more to it than that?"

This time Alex didn't hold back; she rolled her eyes and laughed. "That might work with a twenty-something twit, but I know better than to think you'd call a little over an hour ago to invite me to dinner if all you wanted was a pretty girl sitting across the table from you."

"You're somethin' else, aren't you?" Rory laughed, but then something distracted him, and he scowled. "Incoming," he muttered.

Alex turned around and saw Maddox heading to their table with Miss Bottled-Blonde, trailing after him.

"Rory, good to see you. And, Alex, I thought that was you from behind, although I'm shocked. You never sit with your back to the door."

Maddox shook Rory's hand and leaned in to kiss Alex. She thwarted his aim at her lips by turning quickly, so his kiss landed on her cheek instead. "Gorgeous dress, baby," he whispered before straightening back up.

"You both remember Lena, right?"

Lena stepped forward.

"That's right, your roommate. How's that going anyway?"

"Better than I ever dreamed," answered Lena, not making any attempt to shake Alex's hand. "Maddox, shall we let these two lovebirds be?" Lena grasped his hand, and led him in the direction of their table.

"That was entertaining." Rory smirked.

If Maddox weren't seated at a table on the other side of the dining room, Alex would excuse herself and never come back. As it was, if she left now, Maddox would think it was because of him.

"Cut the crap, Rory. This is quickly becoming one of the most unpleasant evenings I can remember. There's a reason you wanted to have dinner with me. What is it?"

"Okay, if that's the way you want to play it. I hear Los Cab is in serious trouble."

14

"Maddox can't take his eyes off you, by the way."

"I don't care, and it's none of your business. Back to Los Cab, I know how the rumor mill works around here, Rory. I've been part of the Westside Winery Collaborative a long time, and so has my family. You're a newcomer who's taking over a winery that hasn't been in the collaborative's good graces *ever.* I suggest you consider leaving whatever gossip you may have right at this table."

"I'm trying to help, Alex. Calder Wines is in a position to make your family a very attractive offer."

"You've got to be kidding."

"I assure you, I'm not."

Maddox or no Maddox, Alex couldn't be around Rory Calder a minute longer. She picked up her glass of wine, downed what was left in it, grabbed her bag, and walked out.

—:—

"Excuse me," Maddox said to Lena, and followed Alex out of Il Conti.

She was halfway down the block already, and he was right behind her.

"Hold up, there," he hollered. "I thought you were supposed to be taking it easy."

"Leave me alone, Maddox," she hollered back.

If anything, she picked up her pace, forcing him to run after her. When he caught up, he put his hands on her shoulders, forcing her to slow down.

"I didn't leave because of you."

"I know you didn't. I could tell you were unhappy when I approached the table."

"My day for assholes."

Maddox smiled. "Present company excluded of course."

"No, you're an asshole too. You didn't even let your sheets cool off before you reheated them."

"If you're referring to Lena, we're on as much of a date as you and Rory were."

"Maybe now, since you've left her alone at the table."

"No, not before either. It's business, and that's it."

"Awfully romantic restaurant you chose to conduct business."

Maddox shook his head and laughed. "What you do to me, girl."

Alex folded her arms. "Me? Don't you mean Lena?"

Maddox stopped Alex from walking any farther and spun her around to look at him. If she'd only let him, he could drown in the deep, dark pools of her eyes. He gripped the back of her neck and held her still. "No, Alex. Not Lena." He brought his lips to hers, and wasn't gentle about it.

She tried to move away, but he held her tight, and within moments, her arms circled his waist, and her tongue tangled with his. He continued his attack on her mouth until he was breathless and wanted nothing more than to take her into the alley and ravage her. He couldn't though, for a lot of reasons.

Lena was waiting for him, and as much as he didn't want to go back to Il Conti, he had to.

He also heard what Alex had said yesterday, and gave it a lot of thought. She believed they were bed-buddies and nothing more. What she wanted, that he hadn't been smart enough to give her, was romance. She didn't think he was forever material? He'd prove her wrong. But he had to do it his way, or Alex wouldn't believe he was sincere, or that it would last.

Maddox pulled back, and Alex rested her head against his chest. "I wish you wouldn't drive when you're so tired, Al."

"How do you know I drove?"

Maddox nodded his head in the direction of her car, which was visible in the lot across the street. He ran his hands down her back until he reached her bottom, and pulled her closer. "I sure do like this dress."

"I didn't wear it for Rory, or for you. I wore it for me."

He laughed. "Not a surprise, darlin'."

"I need to go, Maddox."

"I wish I didn't have to go back to the restaurant, but I do."

"I'm on my way out of town anyway."

"You are?"

She pulled back from him and took his hands in hers. "I'm going away, Mad. I haven't figured out how long I'll be gone yet. At least a week, but probably longer."

"Where to?"

"I'm not sure, but when I figure it out, my mom and Peyton will know where I am and how to get in touch with me. Otherwise, I need some time off the grid."

"I'm gonna miss you. You know that, right?"

Alex let go of his hands and backed away. "I'm sure I'll run into you when I get back. We can't seem to avoid each other."

"Bye, Al."

She blew him a kiss, turned around, and walked to her car.

Maddox would give anything not to have to go back to Il Conti, but again, he couldn't just leave Lena sitting there. Something told him this getaway of Alex's was significant, though.

"Wait," he called out to her and ran across the street to where her car was parked.

"Maddox, *please*. Just let me go."

"I can't, Alex. Where are you going now? Are you going to Los Cab, or are you going home?"

"Home. I need to pack."

"Give me an hour and a half, and I'll meet you there."

"No, Maddox. Go have dinner with Lena, and I'll see you in a couple weeks."

"I'll be at your place in a little over an hour, Al."

She shook her head and got in the car.

Lena would just have to understand that whatever she wanted to talk to him about was going to have to wait. Alex was more important.

Maddox stopped on his way back in and talked to the waiter to arrange for an order to go. When he walked back into the dining room to let Lena know he had to leave, Rory Calder was sitting in his seat at the table. He seemed very comfortable, but Lena didn't. Their exchange reminded him that they both denied knowing each other when they'd met at the Sea Chest, but something told him that wasn't the case.

"There he is now." Rory stood when Maddox approached the table. "Trouble in paradise?"

Maddox shook his head.

"Rory was just leaving," Lena told him.

"Actually, I thought I'd join you. If you don't mind, Maddox."

Something weird was going on between these two, but Maddox didn't have time to think about that right now.

"As a matter of fact, I've got something pressing I need to take care of—"

"Does this have something to do with the trouble at Los Cab?"

"No idea what you're talking about."

"Rumor is they've got a bond issue."

Maddox did his best not to react, but inside he was reeling. Could the wine stored in his caves belong to Los Cab? "I'm going to give you some friendly advice, Calder. The westsiders are a tight-knit group. If one of our fellow winemakers is in trouble, we come together to help them in a private way. I strongly suggest you don't mention anything to do with Los Cab, or any other winery affiliated with the collaborative, in a derogatory way ever again."

"As I told Alex, Calder Wines is in a position to make them a very generous offer."

"Let me guess, she shut you down the same way I'm about to?"

Maddox could've sworn Rory snickered, but at this point, it didn't matter. All he cared about was getting out of the restaurant and on his way to Alex's.

"Lena? Can I walk you out?" Maddox offered.

She shrugged, and once again, he caught an odd look pass between her and the man she said she didn't know very well. Maybe they were in some kind of cahoots.

"How about we chat another time?"

When she nodded, and he saw the waiter motion for him to come into the bar, Maddox left.

—:—

Alex thought about leaving tonight, just so she wouldn't have to deal with Maddox, but she was almost too tired to drive to Cambria, let alone head north.

Before she made plans to leave, she also needed to talk to Peyton.

Got a minute? She texted.

Peyton answered twenty minutes later. *Of course.*

Gotta get outta Dodge for a bit.

Whatever you need to do. How long?

At least two weeks.

Not a problem.

Alex was beginning to feel like shit about leaving. Neither she nor Peyton had been putting in enough time at Stave. Fortunately they'd been in business long enough that it could roll along on its own.

You sure?

Do what you need to do. No wine dinners until fall. I'm good.

There were several years when they didn't hold wine dinners in the summer because the wineries and restaurants were busy with tourists anyway.

Thanks, Peyton.

Are we okay?

Always.

Earlier, Alex had walked away, leaving Peyton standing in her front yard. Just like Stave had been in business long enough to withstand its two managers taking some time away, she and Peyton had been friends long enough that Peyton would know when Alex needed some slack.

Twenty minutes later, Alex heard Maddox's truck pull in her driveway. That was quick. Did he make Lena take her dinner to go?

She met him at the front door when she saw his arms were full. "What's all that?"

"Dinner. You left Il Conti without ordering, and I figured you'd be hungry."

It was sweet and unlike him. Maddox was always polite—Sorcha raised him to be—but thinking of little things like her being hungry wasn't part of his *modus operandi*.

"I ordered spinach-goat cheese ravioli for you, with a salad, and a veal shank for me. We can share if you'd like."

Alex studied him for a minute. "What's going on?"

"With what?"

"You."

—:—

I want to woo you, he wanted to say, but didn't. If this was going to work, Maddox had to change. A strong word, but that's what he had to do. At the very least, it was time he grew up.

"Not a thing. I was hungry, figured you would be, too."

"What happened to the guy who's been *baching* in too long?"

"You told me earlier that today was your day for assholes. I figured tonight I'd try hard not to be one."

Alex removed the take-out containers from the bag and preheated the oven. She got placemats, plates, silverware, and napkins out of the cupboards and drawers, and set them on the bar in the kitchen.

Maddox walked over to the closet he knew she'd converted for wine storage, and pulled out a Castoro Charbono.

"I was drinking the Pear Valley earlier."

"Yeah, I know."

"Of course you do." Alex rolled her eyes.

"What? I could see it when I walked up to the table."

"So observant."

"That's one thing I don't have to change."

She stopped in the midst of putting silverware on one of the placemats. "What do you have to change, Mad?"

Shit. He hadn't meant to say it that way. "Nothin'."

"No, please, elaborate."

"I don't want to talk about this right now."

"Why not?"

"Because I don't."

"Then you can leave."

"It's going to sound stupid."

Alex raised an eyebrow, which made them both smile.

"I've decided it's time I grew up. Okay? That's it."

"Interesting."

"That's what I figured you'd say."

"Why, Mad?"

He opened the bottle of wine, poured two glasses, and sat on the stool near the bar.

"Because it's time. I'm the oldest in my family, Al. That's big. Just like Gabe, after my father, I'm the patriarch." He rubbed his eyes. "Kade was a real-life hero. There isn't a single one of us that didn't believe our big brother was capable of anything. There also wasn't a single one of us who didn't rely on him in some way."

Alex took a sip of wine and nodded.

"Maybe the girls didn't. I don't know what their relationship with him was like, but Naught, Brodie, and me? We worshiped the ground he walked on. We also went to him for answers to every one of our problems."

"Now you think it's up to you to fill the void."

"Isn't that what Gabe does for all of you?"

Alex didn't answer right away. She got up and put the containers of food in the oven, took another drink of wine, and sat back on the stool.

"Maybe at one time, but lately, today in fact, he was the biggest asshole in my day. I don't know what's going on with him."

"Calder said he heard there was a bond issue."

"There is, but I don't know how Rory knows about it. Gabe insists it isn't that big of a deal, and they'll sort it out. I don't think that's all there is, though."

"What else?"

"He's really impatient with all of us. Which reminds me, did he ever get in touch with you?"

"Damn, that's another thing I keep forgetting to do. I need to call him back. What's he want to talk to me about?"

"That's the thing. He came by Stave, didn't say as much as hello to Peyton and me, and then demanded I tell him where you were. When I told him I didn't know, he left."

"Are you sure this bond issue isn't bigger than you think?"

"How would I know? When I tried to discuss it with him, he got nasty."

"Nasty how?"

"He said he'd start treating me with respect once I started acting like someone worthy of it. Those weren't his exact words, but close enough."

"You're one of the most capable people I know, Al. How could your brother not see that?"

She shrugged her shoulders. "I guess my point is, Gabe isn't the same kind of man you and your brothers are. You may feel the need to fill the role you think

Kade once had, but instead of just taking that on, talk to your siblings about how you're feeling."

"Yeah?"

"If Gabe would tell me what's going on, maybe I could help. Instead, he doesn't just shut me out; he pushes me away. Maybe he is trying to be our 'papa' and take care of whatever it is on his own, but that isn't what I want from him, and I doubt my brothers do either."

"Thanks, Al."

"For what?"

"For giving me a different perspective. One that makes sense."

She smiled again. "You're welcome, Maddox."

The timer buzzed, and she took the containers out of the oven. Maddox took the lids off, brought the plates over, and dished a little of each for both of them.

"This is nice, Mad."

"It is. Thanks for letting me come over."

—:—

It wasn't as though she and Maddox had never had a meal together. They did all the time, but this felt different though. Maybe it was because they were at her house, but it seemed like more than that.

"Where are you goin'?" he asked.

"Not sure yet. Heading north, and from there, I'll wing it. Napa, Sonoma, Calistoga, Russian River."

"Sounds nice. Wish I could join you."

Alex smiled. "Maybe next time."

"Gonna be pretty busy the next twelve months."

"That's right." Alex punched his arm. "I have to hear about the Old Creek property from someone else? What the heck, Mad?"

"I'm sorry, and believe me, there hasn't been anyone I've wanted to talk to about it more than you. I've been leaving a trail of breadcrumbs of things I want to show you."

Alex felt her cheeks grow warm. "Really?"

"Yeah, really. I've only spent part of two days there, but I've already stumbled on some amazing things."

"Like what?"

"Nope. Not tellin'. You wanna know, you gotta come visit."

Was he really living on the property with Lena? It sounded that way. Otherwise, what would there be for her to visit? "No thanks."

"What?" Maddox held his chest. "That wounds me, woman. Why won't you come visit?"

"Think about it, Mad. I'll give you one guess."

She could tell the moment he figured it out, and smiled at the look on his face.

"Here's the deal. Lena's mother died a couple of years ago. She had Parkinson's, and Lena had moved in with her parents to help care for her. When her mother died, her father left, and she's been living there alone since."

"Why doesn't she leave? Don't you own it now?"

"I do, and that night at the Sea Chest, she asked me if she could rent it back from me until she figures out where she wants to go and what she wants to do."

"Where's her dad?"

"No idea."

"Mysterious."

"Right?"

"She bugs me, and not just because of you, Maddox. There's something about her…"

"I know. She seems…I can't come up with the word. Weird." Maddox leaned over and touched her face. "You had some basil…"

"Thanks," she murmured.

His finger lingered and brushed across her lips.

"Alex…"

"I can't, Maddox. That's the thing. We always do this." Maybe now would be a good time to tell him what Gabe said.

"Alex—"

"No, Maddox." She jerked away from him. "Don't do this."

"What am I doing?"

"If you're here for sex, it isn't happening."

"When was the last time I spent the night with you?"

"I don't know."

"Two nights ago. Did we have sex?"

"No."

"No. We didn't, and we're not going to tonight, either."

"Are you leaving?"

"No, I'm not. You are. Tomorrow. And I'm gonna miss the crap out of you."

Maddox helped her clean up the handful of dishes they used, and then looked through her fridge.

"What are you doing?"

"Seein' what I should take home with me."

"You're kidding."

"Why would we let all this great stuff go to waste, Al?"

He made her smile. Gabe was wrong; there was more to this thing with Maddox than just her chasing after him, along with whatever else he was going to say before she slapped him.

—:—

The next morning, Maddox let Alex drive away first, and watched her car until it reached the end of the road and turned on Moonstone Beach Road.

Something felt off, deep inside him, like the last thing he should do was let her drive away.

15

They had two to three weeks before veraison began, and while there wasn't much for Maddox to do in the winery, Naughton would have a hard time staying away from the Butler Ranch vineyards too long.

Once the berries on the vines began changing from green to their harvesting color, and from hard to soft, the countdown to harvest began.

Each grape variety ripened at a different rate, so veraison occurred over a long period of time. Sauvignon Blanc was almost always the earliest ripening grape, and Cabernet Sauvignon tended to be the last. However, regardless of the varietal, veraison typically signaled the six-week countdown to the first harvest.

Where are you? Naughton texted.

Stayed with Alex. Headed home now.

Meeting at Old Creek?

Yep. Time?

Here waiting.

There in ten minutes tops.

Today their plan was to discuss which options were best for which vineyards in terms of *Vitis labrusca* and *Vitis vinifera*. *Labrusca* were grape breeds native to North America; *vinifera* were native to Europe.

When Maddox pulled in, Naught was unloading Huck and Shazam from the trailer.

"Thought we'd ride instead of walk today?"

"Lotta ground to cover."

"Think we'll stumble on anything important riding instead of walking?"

Naughton shrugged. "No tellin'."

Hadn't they walked every square inch of this property yet? Maddox was beginning to think the mystery of whatever it was Kade alluded to in his letter was a joke between his brothers to see if they could drive him crazy.

—:—

Driving away while Maddox sat in his truck and watched was harder than Alex thought it would be. How much nicer would it have been to spend the day with him? He'd been so gentle with her last night, making sure he didn't bump against her in a way that would hurt the parts of her body that were healing.

This morning they'd made breakfast. Maddox had packed away the food in her fridge to take home with him, and then they'd sat and talked until she decided if she didn't leave then, she never would.

He made her promise to call and tell him where she was staying tonight, and every night after that.

"We don't talk every day, Maddox."

"Is there a reason why we can't?" he'd asked.

She'd shrugged her shoulders then, but now, the more she thought about it, the weirder it seemed. Why the sudden move toward a relationship that was more of a …relationship?

Was it because he was afraid she was really going to find someone else and he'd lose his bed-buddy status, or did it mean he actually wanted more than sex with her?

She had miles and hours ahead of her to ponder those questions, but part of getting away was not thinking about Maddox or Stave, or even whatever was going on at Los Cab. This trip was about carving out time for herself.

By the time she got to Carmel, Alex was having a hard time keeping her eyes open. Rather than make the hour-long drive to Big Sur today, she considered stopping for the night. She pulled into the L'Auberge valet and was immediately greeted at her door.

"Ah, *mademoiselle* Alex, *bienvenue*. It is so good to see you."

"Bonjour, Vivienne. Comment allez-vous?"

"Très bien, merci. Et vous?"

"I'm well, thank you."

Vivienne's family had lived in the valley for many years before taking over L'Auberge last year. Alex hadn't visited since they had, but everything looked beautiful. She peered out at the courtyard, full of beautiful pots of flowers.

"Will you stay with us this evening?"

"If you have a room available."

"Oui. The best."

Vivienne's brother, César, fetched Alex's bag from her car. Alex waved. "Hey, César."

"He'll park your car in the garage," Vivienne said as she led Alex to the elevator. When the door opened to the top floor, Vivienne led her down to the end of the hallway and into a suite with a view of the ocean.

"C'est beau, n'est-ce pas?"

"Oui, but know if you continue speaking in French, you'll lose me. I'm very rusty."

Alex met Vivienne in high school, in a French class. It had to have been the easiest grade Vivienne ever received.

"How long will you stay with us?"

"I'm not sure. Do you have guests arriving soon?"

"Not until next week. Please join me in the courtyard for a glass of wine after you're settled."

Vivienne closed the door behind her, and Alex climbed onto the king-size bed. From where she sat, she could see the ocean both through west- and south-facing bay windows.

She checked her phone. There were no texts or messages, but there was an email from her youngest brother, Rascon. Evidently, her mother had called him about her surgery. Maybe she should call and see if he'd talked to Gabe or Enzo.

"Hey, Alex," Rascon answered her call. "How the hell are ya, big sister?"

Alex laughed. "I'm good. I just got your email."

"We haven't heard from you in ages. We were beginning to think you forgot you had a couple of younger brothers."

"You sound like a Texan, Rascon. I haven't forgotten about you. How could I?"

"What about me?" asked Salazar.

It sounded as though Rascon had put the call on speaker.

"You, either. Where are you, guys?"

"Headed to Sonoma for the Wine Country Rodeo."

"I'm not far from you. I'm in Carmel."

It was hard to keep track of where her brothers were this time of the year. July was known in rodeo circles as Cowboy Christmas because there were so many events taking place. If a cowboy got on a roll, he could rack up most of the earnings he'd need to get him to regional finals, and ultimately to the National Finals Rodeo in Las Vegas.

"Why don't you come up?"

"I'll see. Might be hard to find a room."

"You can always stay in the trailer with us."

"Uh, yeah. That won't be happening."

There were a couple of wineries she knew with guest houses. Maybe she'd play her industry card to stay in one for a night or two.

"I'll let you know when I figure it out. Hey, as long as I have you on the phone, have you heard from Gabe or Enzo lately?"

"Not a word. Why?"

"Just wondering. When do you get in?"

"First round isn't until the beginning of next week. Thought we'd get there early and taste some wine. Come up whenever you want, it'll be good to see you."

Alex said goodbye, hung up, and closed her eyes. After the long drive, she needed a nap.

The sun was almost setting when she woke up hungry. She changed out of her now-wrinkled shorts and shirt, put on a sundress and a pair of sandals, and went downstairs in search of Vivienne and a glass of wine.

Wine, cheese, fruit, and a baguette were waiting in the lobby. Alex poured a glass of the unmarked rosé, made herself a plate, and went to sit in the courtyard. There was a library on the other side of the lobby, so after finding a secluded spot to leave her wine and food, she went in search of a book.

When she returned, a few minutes later, she saw she wasn't alone any longer. She couldn't see his face, but the shoulders of the man seated with his back to her were enough to draw her attention.

Just as she sat, he turned around and raised his glass. "You must be Alex," he said.

"I am. Who are you?"

"Vivienne told me to look for you earlier." The man rose and walked to where she sat. "I'm Noah Ridge. My friends call me Ridge, though."

"It's a pleasure to meet you. I might be up near your family's winery next week."

He smiled at her recognition. "On what occasion?"

"My two youngest brothers, Salazar and Rascon, are competing at the rodeo in Sonoma."

"What event?"

"Team-roping. Are you a fan of rodeo?"

"More than a fan. I'm a retired competitor."

Interesting. Alex studied him. What would be his event? He didn't look like a bull rider; he was too tall. Bronc rider maybe?

"Bareback riding."

"That was my guess. Or saddle."

"I'm pleased you'll be there. I'd offer to get you tickets, but I'm sure your brothers will take care of those. Where are you staying?"

"I'm not sure yet."

Ridge reached into his pocket and pulled out a card. "You're welcome to one of the cottages at the winery. Let me know what day you plan to arrive, and I'll make sure it's ready for you."

"That's so kind, but—"

"If you're about to turn down my offer, I can assure you, you'll be hard-pressed to find a place to stay at all, let alone one as nice as this." When Ridge smiled, Alex smiled back.

They'd been chatting for a while when Vivienne came into the courtyard and asked if they were interested in having dinner in Aubergine.

"I don't have dinner plans this evening, do you, Alex?"

"I don't, but Aubergine sounds lovely."

—:—

Maddox had a copy of the property map in his pocket, and asked Naughton if he'd be up for looking at potential building sites.

When he grinned but didn't answer, Maddox knew he'd finally stumbled on Kade's surprise.

Naughton led Maddox over a ridge and stopped Huck when he reached the other side. When Maddox stopped next to him, Naughton pointed.

"This is the only place I've found so far where you can see it."

Maddox looked in the direction Naught pointed, and saw what looked like a building obscured by a grove of trees. "What is it?"

"Let's find out."

16

It took them twenty minutes to ride the trail down from the ridge and then up the opposite hill.

"You okay?" Naughton asked.

"I'm stunned, that's for damn sure."

The building he saw through the trees was actually three buildings. With the use of limestone, travertine, and terracotta tiles on the roofs, all three looked as though they'd been transported straight out of Tuscany.

A beautiful, travertine, cobblestone driveway narrowed into a pathway that wound into a courtyard edged with wrought iron. Planters, made of the same color terracotta tile used on the roofs, were scattered around the space, and there was a fountain Maddox hoped he'd be able to make operational.

The planters were full of lavender, nasturtiums, rosemary, thyme, and sage. While each was overrun, it wouldn't take much work to tame them back to what Maddox envisioned was their original beauty.

Climbing roses and vines that looked more like hops than grapes grew up the sides of the pale-mustard textured stucco, adding vibrant oranges, and contrasting white to the deep green of the leaves. The citrus-floral scent from the flowers took Maddox straight back to the summer months of the year he spent in Europe.

They tethered the horses out of the heat under a canopy of olive and cypress trees, and Naughton found a spigot with running water.

"Weirder and weirder," he mumbled. "Ready to go inside?"

Maddox nodded. "Although I think I could be perfectly happy spending the rest of my life right in this spot."

"It might get better."

Heavy wooden doors ordained with the same wrought iron used in the courtyard led into each of the buildings. Going inside, they found sixteen-foot ceilings supported by massive, rustic, dark wooden beams, in what looked as though it had housed the main winery.

There was ample room in the open space for grape processing, along with barrel and cold storage, fermentation rooms, and even a distillery. There was also an office, lab, and scale room.

They went back outside and walked over to the adjacent building that appeared to be unfinished.

"Tasting room?" Naught asked.

"No idea, but that would be my guess."

It was a gorgeous start, with the same high ceilings and wooden beams found in the main winery, textured walls, and plenty of space to put in a tasting bar, tables, chairs, wine storage, and a retail sales area.

Maddox followed Naughton back outside and to the final structure.

The third set of doors led inside to a foyer, where a dramatic and open staircase with a wrought iron railing went to a second floor.

The right side of the foyer opened to a large sitting room with a dramatic view of the vineyards. To the left was an open kitchen and what appeared to be a grand dining room. The room was lined with windows, all of which looked out over the Pacific Ocean.

Old lemon pots and sizable antique jars that held plants long dead, sat on floors that varied from room to room, made either from wood planks or travertine cobblestone.

Maddox found a small bathroom, but no bedrooms on the main level. At one time, the house may have belonged to Lena's parents, but without any bedrooms on the main level, it would've been completely impractical for them to live in once her mother's illness progressed.

"How did you keep this a secret?" Maddox asked.

"I've never been in it."

They turned the corner and came upon another open staircase, leading down to a basement.

"Now we know how the barrels were moved into the caves."

The basement of the main house appeared to be connected to the two other buildings through a series of tunnels. A conveyor system large enough to move barrels of wine led to what had to be another entrance to the caves.

There were large doors, similar to the alley doors on the barn at Butler Ranch, that opened to another cobblestone pad and, beyond, to a single-lane dirt road.

"Where does that go?" Maddox asked.

"No idea, but we'll know soon."

Maddox looked where Naught pointed and saw Lena's Mercedes CLS400 barreling toward them.

—:—

"I have enjoyed our conversation this evening very much, Alex."

"I have too, Ridge. Thank you." She laughed. "Doesn't it get confusing? Ridge from Ridge?"

He laughed too. "Only my friends call me Ridge. Everyone else calls me Noah. How long will you be here at L'Auberge?"

"I'm not sure, maybe a couple more days. I was headed to Post Ranch Inn today, but was too tired to keep driving, so I stopped to see Vivienne and her family."

"What a coincidence. I'm here for two more days, and then heading to Post Ranch myself."

Ridge had told her, earlier, he handled wine sales for his family's winery, which must've been the reason he was at L'Auberge and also headed to Big Sur.

"Maybe we can have dinner again."

"I'd like that." As much as Alex wanted to get away from wine industry talk, Ridge didn't dwell on it, and neither did she.

"What are you doing tomorrow?" he asked.

"No idea."

"I have meetings in the morning, but I planned to visit Mission Carmel, and then Point Lobos in the afternoon. I'd love it if you'd join me."

"Sounds nice."

Ridge walked her to the elevator. "I'm on this floor, so I'll say goodnight."

"Thank you again for dinner."

"It was my pleasure, Alex Avila. I'll see you tomorrow afternoon."

Alex swooned when the elevator door closed behind her. Noah Ridge was exactly the type of man to help her forget all about Maddox Butler.

—:—

"You found it." Lena climbed out of the car and walked over to where they stood. "What do you think?"

Maddox turned in a circle, looking out at the different vistas.

"Did you live here?"

"No, and neither did my parents. No one has since my grandfather died."

"This belonged to your grandfather?"

"It did, and back in the day, it was really something. I have such wonderful memories of this place. It's been years since I've come up here."

Lena's eyes were misty, but behind her tears, Maddox saw happiness, something he hadn't seen before today.

"How old were you the last time you were in any of these buildings'?"

"I was thirteen when my grandfather died, so shortly before that. He was very ill at the end, and my parents kept me away from him."

"That must've been rough."

"It was, but it had to have been far worse for my mother. It wasn't long before he died that she learned she had Parkinson's too. Watching his final days must've been like looking into her future. I think that's why she never wanted to live in this house."

"It belonged to your mother's parents?" Naught asked.

"Yes. It's odd that everyone always calls it the Hess estate. Even my father never knew how it got started."

"What was your mother's maiden name?" asked Maddox.

"Demetrius. When I was growing up, this estate was called Demetria."

There it was. He knew it as soon as he heard it. *Demetria.* That would be the name of his and Naught's new winery. He looked over at Naughton, who clearly had the same idea.

"Lena, how would you feel—"

"I'd love it."

"How did you know what I was going to ask?"

"It's perfect, Maddox. What else would you name it?"

Before she left them to continue exploring, Lena invited them to dinner the next night, and promised to show them photos of how the estate looked back when it was an active winery.

"I bet she has great stories," Naught said on their ride back along the dirt road.

Maddox nodded. He remembered thinking, just a couple of days ago, that this land might be cursed. Instead, he saw it more clearly now—it was blessed. A gift from his brother. A gift from heaven.

—:—

Shortly after Alex woke up the next morning, she heard a rap at the door.

"Just a minute, please." She pulled on the downy, white robe that hung in the closet, and opened the door.

"Bon matin!" sang Vivienne, who was holding a tray laden with fresh-brewed coffee in a French Press, what Alex knew were fresh croissants, and fruit.

"Alas the rose is not from me, Alex. It is from your not-so-secret admirer."

"Really?" Alex grinned.

"*Oui. Monsieur* Ridge brought it to me this morning in this beautiful bud vase, and asked that it be delivered with your breakfast."

"Wow. It's so…so…"

"Romantic, *n'est-ce pas*? Do you know the meaning of a coral rose, Alex?"

Alex shook her head, still staring at the rose.

"Le désir du cœur."

Alex raised her eyebrows and felt the heat in her cheeks.

"The heart's desire. What did you talk about at dinner last night, *mon amie*?" Vivienne winked.

"I have no idea," Alex murmured, following Vivienne to the table by the window where she set the tray.

"*Bon appétit.* I'll see you later?"

"Yes, and thank you so much, Vivienne."

"It appears the pleasure is all yours, my friend," she said before closing the door behind her.

Alex walked over to the bedside table and picked up the romance novel she began reading last night. She'd only read a handful of pages when she fell asleep, but it would be the perfect accompaniment to her breakfast this morning.

Her phone pinged.

Missed you last night, said the text from Maddox.

She hadn't seen the one he sent the night before, asking her to call before she went to bed.

Not knowing what to reply, Alex didn't. If she was going to move on from her dead-end relationship with Maddox. He couldn't text her every day, and if he did, she wouldn't answer.

Mid-morning, Alex went down to the courtyard and sat in the sun, reading her book. When had she last felt this relaxed? She got lost in her book until Ridge sat in the chaise next to her.

"You're turning pink, Alex."

"You're back early." Alex looked at her phone, astonished to see it was already one in the afternoon. "Wow. I guess you're not back early."

"Good book?"

"Hmm? Yes, it's very good." She fanned the pages. "I can't remember the last time I read more than half-way through a book. This one, I might actually finish."

"Would you prefer to skip our afternoon excursion and finish your book?"

"No, not at all." She set the book on the table. "It'll give me something to do tomorrow."

Ridge smiled.

"What?"

"I may have a few ideas to keep you busy."

"Oh, really?"

"Does the Monterey Bay Aquarium or Seventeen Mile Drive interest you?"

"Maybe. Let's see how our adventures go this afternoon. By the way, thank you for the rose this morning."

"You're welcome. I noticed you had a glass of rosé yesterday afternoon. I thought the color suited you."

"Oh." Alex was mortified that she'd thought the rose meant something more. She'd have a word with Vivienne when she saw her too.

"Shall we?" Ridge held out his hand.

"Should I change?"

"No, Alex. I like you very much just as you are."

She smiled. "I meant my clothes." She was wearing a pair of shorts, a tank, and sandals.

"Up to you, but you might want to grab a jacket, in case it gets chilly later."

"Be right back."

Alex thought about taking the stairs rather than waiting for the elevator, but who knew how much walking she and Ridge might do this afternoon. She had to keep reminding herself that her body was far from recovered from her surgery.

When she came back down to the courtyard, she was wearing white capri jeans and a sleeveless, peach silk blouse. Instead of her usual three-inch heels, Alex had put on a pair of patterned, ankle cowboy boots with a low, square heel, comfortable enough to walk in for hours. She'd let her hair down, but didn't bother putting on any makeup since her morning in the sun had given her plenty of color.

Ridge looked her up and down. "Wow!"

Alex smiled and put her arm through his when he offered it.

Vivienne met them on their way out of the courtyard, carrying a large picnic basket and a blanket. "Anything else I can get you?" she asked Ridge.

"Can't think of a single other thing I'll need," Ridge answered Vivienne, but his eyes never left Alex's.

Vivienne's brother held the door of the deep gray, F-type, convertible Jaguar open for her, but after she was seated, Ridge closed it behind her.

"Nice car," she said when he came around and sat in the driver's seat.

"Thanks. It makes the long sales trips a little more fun."

"I'll say." Alex ran her hands over the rich, deep tan leather that reminded her of her favorite saddle. She'd never been very interested in cars. She had a BMW 4 Series, but only bought it because she liked Peyton's. Hers was light gray; Peyton's was black. Otherwise, they were identical.

"So Alex…"

"Yes, Ridge."

"How much do you know about roses and what the different colors are said to mean?"

"Quite a bit, actually. At least about coral-colored roses."

17

"What the hell is your problem?" Naughton grumbled.

"Nothing," he answered, but that was about as far from the truth as it got.

Alex hadn't answered the text he sent last night, the one he sent this morning, or the one he sent an hour ago. He considered asking Peyton if she'd heard from her, but decided that would make him feel like more of a pussy than he already did.

Maddox spent most of the day in the winery while Naughton worked with the vineyard crews. He was happy for the peace and quiet, and took his time inspecting the equipment that was already there, making lists of what might work, what needed to be repaired, and what needed to be replaced. Everything was old, but that didn't necessarily mean it wasn't as good, or better, than what he'd replace it with.

"Goin' home," Naughton snarled as he walked out of the winery.

"See ya later?"

"Nah. I'll see you tomorrow."

"Wait." Maddox followed Naughton outside. "Aren't you coming to dinner with Lena?"

"Not interested."

"She said she'd show us photos of how this place looked back in the day."

"Why would I care?"

"I don't know, maybe you'd like to see how some of the vineyards were planted, or their harvesting techniques. Maybe you'd learn something to make dinner worth your while."

"Doubt it. Everything I need to know about the vineyards, I've already seen."

"Do what you want, then. I don't give a shit."

Naughton walked away, shaking his head.

Screw him. Maddox didn't owe him an explanation about why he was grouchier than usual. Naughton was the grouchiest asshole Maddox had ever met, and he never explained himself. He doubted Lena would care whether Naught showed up either. In fact, they still hadn't had the conversation she wanted to have at dinner the other night.

Instead of going home, Maddox closed the doors to the winery and walked over to the house. He still hadn't been on the second floor, so had no idea what to expect.

The first floor had a scattering of furniture in the rooms, tables and chairs mainly, which looked as though they'd been designed specifically for the space they filled. There were two sofas and four upholstered chairs in the sitting room that would either need a deep cleaning, or to be replaced.

The kitchen would need all new appliances, but the cupboards, counters, and floors were sound, and like most everything else, needed to be scoured.

He pulled out a chair and sat at a table large enough to hold sixteen. He liked how the kitchen was open to the dining room, but would add an island to create more of a separation.

Instead of going back downstairs to the basement level, Maddox followed the curve that led back around to the main foyer.

He'd made it halfway up the stairs before he got a feeling he couldn't explain. Whatever it was, it wasn't good. He turned and sat on a step rather than continuing to the second level.

—:—

Ridge parked in the lot adjacent to the entrance to the Carmel Mission. While that was what most called it, the sign at the entrance read "San Carlos Borromeo de Carmelo Mission."

There were very few tourists visiting the mission, so the atmosphere was serene as they walked through the courtyard and gardens.

"My family settled in California before this mission was built," Alex told Ridge.

"Avila Beach have anything to do with your family?" he asked.

"Very much so. My ancestors were *Castellanos* from Castile in central Spain, and arrived in what was known then as *Las Californias*. They settled in the area that became Avila Beach at the same time Father Serra founded the mission in San Luis Obispo."

"You probably know a lot more about missions than I do."

Alex laughed. "You have no idea. My father insisted we attend mass at *Mission San Luis Obispo de Tolosa* every Sunday."

"Impressive accent, Alex, or is it Alexis?"

"Yes, it's Alexis, although no one calls me that except my mother, and that's only when she's mad at me."

"It wouldn't be a good idea for me to call you Alexis, then."

"Only if you want me to call you Noah."

"It wouldn't matter what you called me, Alex. I love the sound of your voice either way."

Alex smiled and looked over at the Basilica Church.

"When Mexico gained control of the region, our family was ostracized. My father told me the stories passed down through his grandfather. We were known as *Californios*. Have you heard that expression before?"

"I haven't. Is it like Chicanos?"

"Similar. Chicanos are from Mexico. Californios are from Spain. Many families, like ours, stopped speaking Spanish completely when they settled here, so the Mexicans called them 'white Spanish.'"

"Do you speak Spanish?"

"Fluently. My mother is Mexican."

"And you're Catholic?"

"My mother is." Alex laughed. "I suppose my brothers and I are too, although I rarely go to mass. I stopped going after my father died."

"Your father was legendary. He's definitely one of my father's heroes."

"You're kidding. Why?"

Ridge put his arm around Alex's shoulders. "Why? You're asking me why someone would idolize one of the greatest winemakers who ever lived?"

Alex wasn't sure if Ridge was being serious or if he was playing with her.

"I love how animated you are when you talk about your family and your heritage. Do you know your accent gets more pronounced when you do?"

"I don't have an accent," she protested.

"Oh, but you do. And it's beautiful. It makes me want to ravage you." Ridge pushed her into one of the alcoves. "Can I kiss you, Alexis? Please? I've been dying to since last night."

Alex nodded her head, and Ridge pressed his lips against hers. His kiss was soft and tentative, hardly ravaging. When she attempted to use her tongue to urge him to be bolder, he pulled back further. Maybe he hesitated because this was their first kiss, but Alex found herself disappointed.

Noah Ridge was handsome, with a great body. Not as good as Mad's body, but she was trying hard not to compare them. He was attentive, interesting, a good conversationalist, and he made her laugh. He was romantic too, and generous. Why did a single kiss have to disappoint her so profoundly?

When he leaned into her and grazed her abdomen, she flinched.

"Are you okay?" he asked, pulling away further.

"I had surgery a couple of weeks ago, and I sometimes forget how sore I am until I move the wrong way."

"I'm so sorry." Ridge pulled her out of the alcove, and they continued their walk through the mission gardens.

"It isn't a big deal," Alex told him, but it didn't do any good. The rest of the afternoon, he rarely touched her, and when he did, it was as though she might break.

Any thoughts she'd had of kissing him again were squashed by his insistence that they talk more about Spanish history.

When Ridge asked if she wanted to continue their afternoon by visiting Point Lobos, Alex suggested they stop and have an early dinner instead. They were near one of her favorite Italian restaurants, and she thought a glass of wine or two might loosen him up a bit.

Their easy conversation resumed over a bottle of Barolo Monfortino and a fabulous garlic-laden dinner.

"Thank you, Alex," he said between bites of lasagna.

"What for?"

"Giving me another chance."

Instead of waiting for him, Alex leaned over and kissed him. She put her hand on the back of his neck and held him close. She teased his lips with her tongue, and this time, Ridge responded. She deepened their kiss, and then pulled back.

"What's wrong?" Ridge asked.

Alex rubbed her chest and leaned back in her chair. "I don't know, maybe the wine is giving me heartburn." A feeling she couldn't explain came over her, as though something bad was about to happen.

—:—

Maddox decided to wait and explore the second floor in the morning. The pain in his chest had subsided, but it was getting close to dinnertime, and he still needed to go home to change.

When he reached the foyer, he turned and looked back at the place he'd sat moments before. The sun shone through the second story window in such a way that only that step was out of the shadows.

He felt warm, and thought about unbuttoning his shirt, but it wasn't that kind of warmth. It was more as though the light that shone on the step also shone on him. A sense of peace washed over him, as though something, or someone, was telling him this was where he belonged. He stayed in one place, basking in the sunlight until it no longer shone through the window.

His phone pinged on the way to his truck, and he saw a text from Lena, asking him to stop by the house now.

Worked in the winery most of the day. Dusty and dirty.

It's okay. Stop anyway.

Lena greeted him at the door and invited him in, and pointed to a hallway. "There's a bathroom on the right if you feel like washing up."

He thanked her and closed the bathroom door behind him. The warm feeling he'd had at the house on the hilltop was replaced with a chill. Maybe he should cut the evening short and get some rest. He felt like he might be getting sick.

When he came back out, Lena had photos scattered on a table near the kitchen. Maddox scanned the sparsely-furnished house. It looked as though she'd been packing. Maybe she'd made some decisions about where she wanted to go and what she wanted to do.

"When I pulled out these photos, I remembered my grandmother used to call the house Casa Gialla." Lena handed him several pictures.

As he shuffled through them, Maddox saw the planters looked as he'd imagined they would if the overgrowth was cleaned up. In one photo, the house looked as though it had originally been a much brighter shade of yellow. He preferred the faded and weathered look it had now.

"I'm leaving, Maddox," she blurted. "It's one of the reasons I asked you to dinner tonight. I wanted to tell you at Il Conti, but—"

"I'm sorry about leaving the way I did."

She shook her head. "Don't be."

"Where are you headed?"

"I'm not certain yet. I'll put what I want to keep in storage. There isn't much of it. And then I plan to travel for a few months."

"Will you see your father?"

Maddox watched as she quickly masked the darkened expression that came with the mention of her father.

"Perhaps…" Lena picked several more photos up from the table and looked through them. "I thought maybe there was one of my parents together, but I haven't been able to find any."

He and Lena both reached for a photo that had fluttered to the floor, but Maddox snapped it up first.

"What's this?" he asked, holding the photo under the light. It was faded, as though it had been left in direct sunlight, but the image was clear enough for him to recognize the two people in the photo. Maddox would guess it was taken about twenty years ago.

"Lena, you never mentioned you knew my brother."

"I more than knew him, Maddox. Kade was my husband."

18

"You know…" Ridge began while they waited for dessert. "I've been thinking about your reaction when I said your father was my father's hero."

"And?" Alex took another sip of her wine.

"He wasn't only renowned for his wine, but the land and vineyards at Los Caballeros are the envy of every landowner I know."

"There are many estates in your area to be envied."

"Not like your family's, though. If your brothers ever thought about getting out of the business and selling, I'm sure the bidding on that property would escalate quickly."

"I don't think that is a remote possibility. Have you heard otherwise?"

"Yes and no. I mean it's no secret that the bigger wineries are anxious to expand into the Central Coast. There have been bidding wars already on several properties."

"Such as?"

"Tablas Creek. I'm sure you've heard Calder Wines recently made that purchase."

"I had heard." Alex didn't try very hard to mask her sneer.

"If that look means what I think it does, I have to admit Rory Calder is not someone I would call a friend."

"There's just something about him." Alex shook the weird feeling away that came whenever she thought about Rory.

"What other properties have been for sale?"

He rattled off several she knew, but hadn't known were for sale.

"Part of the Hess estate, of course."

"Part?" Alex leaned forward and rested her elbows on the table.

"Only the daughter's holdings were available. The rest was part of the divorce settlement. My understanding is her ex-husband recently passed away; however, the land had already been deeded to members of his family before he died. I haven't heard whether they're interested in selling."

Alex's mind was reeling. "Do you know who her ex-husband was?"

"Someone from a wine family. I'm trying to remember; I know I've heard the name." Ridge thought for a minute. "I know, it was your neighbor—the Butler family."

Alex asked a handful of other unrelated questions, and then excused herself. She walked to the ladies' room, trying to wrap her head around what Ridge had just told her. She couldn't decide whom she wanted to call first, Peyton or Maddox, knowing she wouldn't call either of them.

"I told you more about the Hess deal than I should have. All interested parties were required to sign a non-disclosure agreement before we were given the details surrounding the sale," Ridge said when Alex returned to the table.

"Do you know who bought the property?"

"No one. It was withdrawn."

"Any idea why?"

"No clue."

Their dessert of berries and cream went largely untouched as they continued their conversation about property for sale on the Central Coast.

"Ridge, I'm going to ask you a very direct question, one you may feel uncomfortable answering."

"Go ahead."

"You mentioned that Los Cab would be a property of great interest if it was ever for sale. Have you heard anything that would lead you to believe our family might be interested in putting it on the market?"

"Yes, Alex. I have."

"Will you tell me who you heard it from?"

—:—

Maddox got up from the table and walked to the other side of the room, still holding the photograph of Lena and Kade. In it, the two had their arms wrapped around each other, but were facing the camera. Both were smiling.

"Is this what you really wanted to tell me?"

"No. I hadn't planned to."

Maddox didn't know which question to ask first. He could think of so many.

"Why?" he finally asked.

Lena looked away from him. "It wasn't up to me, Maddox."

"What does that mean?"

"I shouldn't have told you. This is very hard for me."

He was speechless. This was hard for her? "You've got to be kidding?" he sneered. "What the hell else is there? What else am I going to find out about my brother?"

"Please, don't—"

"*Don't what? Jesus.* He was my brother." Maddox was so angry, he almost grabbed her. If he had, he would've shaken her until she answered every last one of his questions.

His confusion, his hurt, his anger, and his powerlessness were a boiling mess inside of him. The pain he'd felt in his chest earlier had nothing on the torment he felt in his soul.

Without another word, Maddox walked out the front door, got in his truck, and drove home. The photo of Kade and Lena sat on the seat beside him.

How was dinner?

Naughton must've seen him pull into the barn. *Changed my mind. Long day. Calling it a night.*

Meeting the crew at dawn. Pick you up at 5.

Maddox didn't answer. He had no idea whether he'd be able to go with Naughton tomorrow, or ever set foot on the property again.

He poured himself three fingers of bourbon and went out the back door and into the vineyards, carrying the glass and bottle with him.

He walked and walked, waiting until his steps were lit only by the moon before he cursed his brother's name.

He'd loved Kade. He'd admired and respected him. He'd always believed he wanted to be just like him, but now he didn't know what that meant. He felt as though he'd lost Kade all over again. His brother wasn't just dead, Maddox's memories had all been obliterated by Kade's subterfuge.

How many times had he railed at the heavens for taking his brother? Now he railed at Kade instead. He sobbed until he could no longer stand, and fell as much as sat on the ground.

Worse than his anger at Kade and the answers to questions that had died when he did, was the terrible burden he now carried.

How would his family feel if they also found out the things he knew about Kade? Would they feel betrayed that he hadn't told them as soon as he knew? Should he go to his parents and ask what they knew? Who else carried Kade's secrets?

He ignored the phone he forgot he had with him when it pinged. Only when the pinging became incessant did he look. Three missed calls. All from Alex. The only person on earth he would even consider talking to.

—:—

As much as Alex wanted to see her two brothers, and as much as she wanted to continue her respite, she couldn't. She had to talk to Maddox, and as hard as it would be, she had to tell him what Ridge had told her.

It was hard to believe, but certainly explained how Kade came to own the land he gave to Maddox and Naughton. There was no possible way Kade could've afforded to buy it outright.

Their car ride home from dinner was quiet. Ridge walked her to her room, but his attempt to kiss her goodnight fell flat.

He murmured something about seeing her the next day, but they both knew Alex's focus was no longer in Carmel. She might as well be home, because that's where her head was.

"Goodnight, Ridge. Thank you for today."

"Goodnight, Alex. I wish I knew what I said right before I lost your attention."

"I'm tired, that's all." She put her hand on his shoulder and kissed his cheek.

She tossed and turned for more than an hour before she finally picked up her phone and called Maddox. It was just after ten, but they often talked later than that. She called, and then called again three minutes later, and two minutes after that.

Just as she was about to call for the fourth time, Maddox called her instead.

"Alex…"

The sound of his voice startled her. Was he drunk?

"Maddox?"

"Where the hell have you been, Al? I need you so much, and you haven't been here."

"I'm coming home tomorrow."

"That might be too late."

"What does that mean?"

Maddox didn't answer. She pulled the phone from her ear and checked the screen. He'd hung up on her.

Why'd you hang up? She texted him, but he didn't respond.

Alex felt sick to her stomach most of the way home. It wasn't just Maddox she needed to tell what Ridge had told her about Kade; she also had to tell Peyton. This wasn't something she could keep secret. If she did and they ever found out she'd kept it from them, they'd feel as betrayed by her as she was sure they were going to feel by Kade.

Not long after Peyton met Brodie, and she struggled with her attraction to him, Alex had told her that Kade wasn't the man Peyton thought he was. It appeared Peyton wasn't the only one who had been deceived. Kade wasn't the man any of them thought he was.

—:—

Maddox opened the door when he heard the knock. He still hadn't gone to bed.

"You ready to leave?" Naught asked.

"I'll have to meet you over there later." Maddox gripped the back of his neck with his hand and rubbed the muscles tight from stress.

"What's goin' on? You been drinkin'?"

His first test. Did he tell Naughton what he'd learned last night, wait, or never tell him? The only thing he knew for sure was he wouldn't tell him now.

"Told you it was a rough night. I'll see you there later."

Naughton shrugged and left, and Maddox paced. He felt like shit for hanging up on Alex last night, and then not answering her text. He looked out the window when he saw the lights of a car barreling down the main drive of the ranch. It looked like a light gray BMW.

—:—

Alex stopped near the barn doors and waited for them to open wide enough that she could drive in. She'd slept for a couple of hours, and when she got tired of tossing and turning, she decided to get on the road. She left a note for Vivienne, along with an envelope for Ridge. She hadn't said much in either, only that there was an emergency at home that necessitated her leaving in the middle of the night. Her only worry was finding her car keys, but she found them on a peg behind the check-in desk.

She spent the two-hour drive going back and forth about whether to tell Maddox what Ridge had told her, ultimately deciding he deserved to know and there was no better person for him to hear it from than her.

He was waiting when she climbed out of the car, and pulled her close to him.

"What are you doing here, Al?"

"You hung up on me, Mad."

"So?"

She had been right last night when she thought he might be drunk. By the look of him, he still was.

"Can we go inside?"

"No. Let's walk instead." Maddox walked back out the barn doors.

"Wait." The sun was just coming up, and it was chilly. She popped the trunk, grabbed a jacket, and raced out of the barn to catch up with him.

He was already a hundred yards ahead of her, and she knew better than to try to run after him.

"Wait for me," she hollered, not sure whether he could even hear her.

He kept walking, and once he crested the edge of the vineyards, she couldn't see him anymore. When she came over the same crest, he was waiting for her.

"Why are you here?" he asked again.

"I need to talk to you about something."

"At dawn?" He started to walk again.

"It's important. Maddox, please, I can't run after you."

He stopped again. "If you're here to tell me we're through, you've found the love of your life, or any other shit related to us, I'm not interested in hearing it."

"I'm not here to talk about us, Maddox."

"Really?"

"It's about Kade."

He spun around and grabbed her by the arms, pulling her close enough to kiss. The stench of whiskey on his breath made her sick to her stomach.

"Whatever you want to tell me about Kade, I don't want to hear." He laughed. "He the love of your life, Al?" he sneered.

"What? Don't be ridiculous—"

"When it comes to my big brother, *nothing* would surprise me. Thought better of you, though."

He still held her close to him. The grip he had on her arms hurt. "Let me go, Maddox."

"Let you go? Sure, sweetheart. Let me give you a kiss goodbye first."

Maddox gripped her chin with one hand while the fingers of his other continued to grip her arm. He moved to kiss her, and when she didn't respond, he jammed his tongue in her mouth. He wasn't kissing her; he was taking out his anger on her lips and her tongue. He was intentionally hurting her.

"Who's the love of your life, Al? Someone who will fuck you better than me? Is he waiting in your bed? Is that why you want me to let you go?"

She wanted to slap him, but as slurred as his words were, she doubted he'd remember any of this once he sobered up.

Maddox pushed her away from him. "Leave. Go. Get the hell out of my sight. Go to him, whoever the hell he is."

"*Maddox, stop this.* There isn't anyone else."

"No? That's funny. You've made it pretty clear I'm not the love of your life."

You are, though, she wanted to tell him, but not like this, not when he was drunk.

"Kade—"

"*Stop!*" he shouted. "I don't want to hear about Kade. Not ever again. Got it?"

"Maddox, please. Let's go back to the house. I'll make you some coffee."

"Leave me alone. I don't want coffee, and I don't want you. How's it feel to hear you're not wanted, Al? Feel pretty good? No? Yeah, I know firsthand."

When she put her hand on his arm, he wrenched away from her.

"Get outta my sight, Alex. I don't want you here. In fact, I never want to see or hear about you again either." Maddox spun around and walked away from her.

Even if she'd wanted to catch him, she wouldn't be able to, but since she didn't want to anyway, she turned around and walked back to the house.

It sounded as though Maddox already knew about Kade's marriage to Lena, but how had he found out? Or, he'd learned something else about his brother that resulted in him getting shit-faced. It wouldn't surprise her if there were more things Kade had kept secret. They may never know it all.

—:—

Shit's gotten weirder. Naught's text said. *Lena's gone and so is the wine.*

Maddox ignored him. He didn't care if the wine was gone, in fact, he was glad it was. And as far as Lena was concerned, if he never saw her again, it would be too soon.

You coming over here or not?

He turned around and walked back to the house. Maybe he'd answer Naughton later, after he had a chance to sleep. Maybe not. Trouble? Who cared? He didn't.

When he got to the top of the hill, he saw the barn doors were open and Alex's car was still inside.

What the hell? Why was she still here? Whatever she wanted to tell him, he didn't want to know. He was sick of hearing her talk about how she had to find the love of her life. What was wrong with him that he couldn't be the love of her life, and Kade had spent his whole life lying to him?

He went in the front door, and Alex was waiting for him on the stairs. "I told you to go away."

"Since when do I listen to you?"

"I don't want you here."

"Yeah, I know."

He stepped forward when she stood and walked toward him. "And I don't want any coffee."

"No coffee, then."

When Alex took his hand, he followed her upstairs, into his bedroom, and then to his bed. She pushed him so he fell backward on the hard mattress.

He let Alex take over, something he rarely did, but he was too drunk to care. He watched as she pulled his shirt over his head, and then worked her way down his body, unzipping his jeans. She moved to his feet, and pulled off his square-toe boots, the ones he only wore when he walked the vineyards or worked in the barns. They smelled like dirt and manure, so when she held them with the tips of her fingers and set them outside the bedroom door, he laughed.

Next, his socks came off. She made her way back to his waist, pulled his jeans and boxer briefs off together, and threw them in the pile with his shirt and socks.

Instead of climbing into bed with him, Alex walked away. He heard water flowing into the tub, and looked her body up and down when she returned naked. He stood when she reached out her hand, and followed her into his favorite room in the house.

Alex climbed into the swirling water first, and Maddox followed. He sank into one of the molded sections of the tub that was built more like a hot tub or spa, and let his head rest on the contours.

Alex was on her knees in front of him, and gently ran her soapy hands over his body. When she finished washing every inch of the front of him, she wiggled her finger for him to follow. She rested in one of the other molded contours, and Maddox sat with his back to her.

After washing his hair, she pulled him close so he rested against her, and softly ran her fingers over his chest. He loved that, and she knew it. She also knew it was the easiest way to lull him to sleep.

Maddox half-slept, aware of her hands softly stroking his skin, and of the water whirling around him, keeping the nausea from too much liquor at bay. The same thoughts plagued him in his stupor. How could this woman, who knew just what he needed, not love him?

He came fully awake when he felt a chill from the receding water.

"Let's get in bed, Mad," she whispered.

He stood and offered his hand to help her stand. She'd set two towels on the edge of the tub, and instead of drying herself first, she dried him.

"Why?"

"Because you're exhausted, and you need to sleep."

"No, Alex. Why can't you love me?"

19

The little sleep he got was plagued by alcohol-induced dreams. In them, Alex left him, saying again she'd found someone else to love. Between the dreams and waking up every five minutes to make sure she was still next to him, he might as well not have slept at all.

He only remembered bits and pieces of their conversation from earlier. She came here because she wanted to tell him something about Kade, but he wouldn't let her. He wasn't sure he'd let her now. How much more was there to learn about the brother he thought he knew so well? How much more could he bear?

He rested his eyes on Alex's beautiful face and her hair that was fanned out on his pillows. She never slept with it loose. It was too long, she'd tell him when he begged her to. "It'll be too hard to brush out," she'd explain, but he remembered asking again, right before he drifted to sleep, and this time, she gave in.

He looked over at his phone on the nightstand, wondering if he should check it or just let it be. Naughton was probably good and pissed at him by now, but he couldn't muster up enough of a shit to give any.

"Hey," Alex murmured groggily.

"Hey." Maddox rested back against the pillow and pulled her naked body close to his.

"How do you feel?"

"Less drunk than I was, but still more than I should be."

Alex picked up her phone. "Naughton called, so has Peyton." Alex rested her head back on his chest. "Should we let the world in yet?"

He sure as hell didn't want to, but the call from Peyton worried him. Had she somehow found out that the man she thought she'd been in love with was a liar? "Did she leave a message?"

"Yeah, but I didn't listen to it."

"What were you going to tell me about Kade?" he didn't want to ask, but he had to.

"Are you sure you want to talk about that now?"

"Yeah, I found out a few things about him myself last night."

"About Kade and Lena?"

Maddox nodded. "So you know. Is there more?"

"No. Just that the land was part of their divorce settlement."

"How'd you find out?"

"Noah Ridge told me. We were talking about land for sale in the valley, and he mentioned the property on Old Creek Road. His family made an offer on 'the daughter's land.'"

"Why were you with Noah Ridge?" Maddox's gut lurched. Was Noah the new man in her life?

"That isn't important—"

"Stop right there. It's important to me. Why, Alex?"

"Coincidence. We happened to be the only two guests at L'Auberge, and had dinner at the same time."

"He isn't the new love of your life?"

Alex sat up in bed. "Look at me," she demanded.

Maddox turned his head and met her eyes. Here it came, and he wasn't sure he was ready. He might never be ready for Alex to tell him she was in love with someone else.

"What are you thinking right now?" she asked.

"Are you kidding? Whatever it is, just say it, Alex." Every muscle in his chest was tight, as though he was trying to protect his heart from the words she was about to speak.

"I kissed Noah last night."

"Jesus, Alex—" Maddox tried to get up, but she laid her body across his.

"Let me finish."

Did she think he didn't have a heart? Or that he was made of steel?

"It felt wrong, Mad. I got this feeling like something was terribly wrong."

So had he. "When?"

"Last night."

"When last night, specifically?"

"I don't know, around six or seven, I guess. Why is that important?"

Because he'd felt it too. That was why he didn't go upstairs, because he'd felt it too. Could he tell her without sounding crazy?

"Why, Maddox?"

"I think I knew."

"How?"

"Like you, it was a feeling."

Alex's eyes filled with tears. "You asked me if Noah's the new love of my life. He isn't. There's someone else I've been in love with since I was a teenager.

Someone I can't stay away from. For a long time, I thought it was just sex between us, but it isn't."

"Are you saying—"

"*You* are the love of my life, Maddox. You. If you can't accept that, then we are done, because I can't live another day knowing I love you, but you don't love me."

"I asked you before we got in bed why you couldn't love me, Al."

"Yes, you did."

"Why didn't you answer me?"

"I wanted to wait until you were sober to tell you I love you."

"I'm not all the way sober yet."

Alex sat up and climbed on top of him, straddling him with her nakedness. She pulled her hair back, twisted it in a makeshift ponytail, and then folded her arms over her breasts.

Maddox reached up, moved her arms away, and covered her breasts with his hands. "How long have you loved me?" he asked.

"Since I met you."

"Same for me."

"Why didn't you—"

"Why didn't you?"

When her eyes filled with tears again, he shifted and rolled her on her back. He laid his body over hers and pinned her hands above her head. "Look at me," he demanded in the same way she had. "What are you thinking right now?"

She smiled. "You're such a jerk."

"It's called torture, Alex, and it's what you've been doing to me."

"I didn't realize."

"I guess I didn't either. Or I did, but I didn't think you felt the same way."

"Me, too."

Who would say it first? After all these years, could either of them swallow their pride enough to finally admit how they felt? Yeah, he could. He brought his face close enough to hers that he could kiss her but still see her eyes. "I love you, Alex."

"I love you, Maddox."

She held him so tight. What he'd give to show her right now how much he loved her, but he didn't want to hurt her.

"Maddox, stop thinking and make love to me," she implored.

Alex knew her own mind and her own body. If she wasn't healed enough, she wouldn't do this.

She pushed at him until he was on his back. "Better this way," she said, before straddling him again, only this time, she made sure he was tucked inside her warmth.

They'd just finished ravaging each other when they heard someone pounding on the front door.

"What the hell?" Maddox yelled.

"Who is that?" she whined and put the pillow over her head.

"Maddox, open the damn door."

"Naughton," they said in unison.

The clothes he had on earlier were filthy from his long day yesterday, and then long night. He opened a dresser drawer, pulled out a clean shirt and a pair of shorts. "Be right back." He stopped to look at her one more time before he went downstairs.

Today was going to be a shit-storm of Kade's deceit. Did Alex know that as long as she was beside him, he felt as though he could make it through the crap that swirled around him?

He pulled open the door. "What's up, Naught?"

"She's gone."

"I know."

"How do you know?"

"You texted me. How do *you* know?"

"I found the door open this morning, and the place empty."

"Empty?"

"What happened at dinner last night?"

Maddox stepped back and motioned for his brother to come in.

"Hey, Alex," said Naughton.

Alex walked up behind Maddox and put her hand on his arm, pulling it away from his neck. "Stop. You're gripping it so hard it's red."

"Thanks," he muttered.

Naughton looked between the two of them, and then leaned up against the wall. "That isn't all."

Maddox tensed his arm, trying to keep himself from rubbing the back of his neck before he rubbed it clear through to his spine.

"You already told me. The wine is gone too."

Did Naughton think Lena took it? And if she did, so what? It wasn't their wine. They'd asked her if she knew who left it in the caves, but she was evasive.

"It might be a good idea to contact Peter Wendt."

"Why?" Naught asked.

"It's complicated."

Naughton looked at Maddox, and Maddox looked at Alex.

"There are questions surrounding how we came to own the property that maybe he can answer."

"He can't." Naught's shoulders drooped forward.

"Why not?"

"He just can't."

"How do you know, Naught?"

"I just know. Let it alone, Mad."

Maddox felt the anger travel through his body. More secrets? "Did you know Kade was married to Lena Hess?" Maddox asked.

"No, I didn't."

"Did you know he got the land he gave us as part of the divorce settlement?"

"No, but it makes sense."

Everything Maddox thought he knew about his brother screamed inside him. Kade never would've taken someone's land in a divorce. Never. But then he never would've believed Kade would marry without his family's knowledge. Or marry at all.

What about Naught? Was his reaction just typical Naughton, or did he know a hell of a lot more than he was letting on?

"Are you sure we even own this land?"

"Yeah, Maddox. We do."

"Are you certain?"

"The deeds are in Kade's safe deposit box."

Kade had a safe deposit box? One that Naughton knew about? Maddox felt like his head was going to explode. Later, when he could get Naught alone, he'd force his brother to tell him everything he knew, even if it meant putting a gun to his head.

"How'd you find out Lena was married to Kade?"

"Come with me." He motioned to both Naught and Alex. He led them out the door and to the barn, where he told them to wait while he got something out of his truck. He grabbed the photo and handed it to Naughton first, who looked at it briefly, and then handed it to Alex.

"It was in with the other photos she showed me. I don't think she intended for me to find out."

"We need to tell Brodie."

—:—

As Alex studied the photo of Kade and Lena, only one thing came to mind—how Peyton was going to feel when she found out about this.

She'd moved on from Kade, fell in love with Brodie, and Alex believed she was far better off, but she'd still probably be hurt and wonder why Kade had never told her. Peyton needed to know about this before word spread, and Alex had to be the one to tell her.

"Can you get Brodie to meet you over there?" she asked Maddox.

"Where? Old Creek Road?"

Alex nodded.

"Probably. Why?"

"You tell Brodie, and I'll tell Peyton."

"Good idea."

Maddox called, and then confirmed Brodie was on his way.

Alex texted Peyton to say she was on her way to her house in Cambria.

Perfect timing, Brodie just left to meet his brothers. Peyton answered.

"All set."

Maddox put his arm around her shoulders. "Thanks, Al." He leaned in closer. "I love you," he whispered.

Alex felt as sick on this drive as she had earlier when she drove back from Carmel. There was no easy way to tell Peyton that Kade had been married when he was younger.

She doubted Peyton would feel as betrayed as Maddox did. Kade was his brother. Finding out he'd been married without anyone in their family knowing had to hurt like hell. She'd be hurt if she discovered one of her brothers married without her knowledge.

"Hey, Jamie." He was out front with Finn, playing basketball, and stopped to hug her.

"Hey to you too, Finn." He did the same thing.

"Your mom inside?"

Both boys nodded, and Alex opened the front door.

"I thought you were out of town?" Peyton walked over and hugged her the same way the boys had.

"I had to come back."

Peyton's expression changed from happy to see her, to concerned. "Why?"

"Have a seat." Peyton sat, and Alex poured a glass of wine from the bottle already open on the counter.

"Kade was married once before, in his twenties. No one knew about it."

Peyton stood, walked to the front of the house, and looked out the window. "Are the boys playing basketball?"

"Yeah. Are you okay?"

"I think so. I'm more worried about Brodie, though. You say no one knew?"

"Mad didn't know, and neither did Naught."

"How did you find out?"

Alex told Peyton about having dinner with Noah Ridge, and how it came up without his realizing her connection to the Butler family.

"And then last night, Lena Hess was showing Maddox photos of the property, and one fell on the floor, of her and Kade. That's when she told him they'd been married. According to Noah, Kade got the land as part of the divorce settlement."

"Lots of secrets," Peyton murmured.

"You sound like Maddox."

"Is he telling Brodie now?"

Alex nodded. "Both he and Naught are."

"I feel like we should go there."

"You do?"

"Yeah, don't you?"

Now that Peyton said it, she did. "What about the boys?"

"I'll call Addy."

Addy worked at Stave. She and their other main employee, Sam, often babysat Jamie and Finn.

Peyton picked up her phone and sent a text. Her phone pinged almost immediately.

"She's on her way."

Peyton's reaction surprised her, but it shouldn't have. Peyton loved Brodie, so she was more worried about him than she was upset that Kade never told her he'd been married.

When Addy got there, Peyton rode to Old Creek Road with Alex since Brodie had driven his truck to meet his brothers.

"I'm worried about Naughton too," she said.

"Yeah. It's impossible to know how he feels about anything."

"Kade told me once that he worried more about Naughton than any of his other siblings."

"Did he say why?"

"He told me it was because Naught held everything inside. He didn't confide in anyone. The reason Kade knew was because it's how he was."

"That's for damn sure," Alex murmured.

—:—

There were chairs by the creek. Maddox had sat in them the other day, while he waited for Naughton to show up. He motioned for his brothers to follow, and that's where he and Naughton told Brodie about Kade, and how they'd come to own the land.

Brodie took it much in the same way Maddox had, but wasn't quite as emotional about it. He was shocked, he had questions, but he wasn't angry.

"You want in?" Naughton asked. It wasn't something he and Maddox had discussed, but it made sense to make Brodie the offer.

Brodie thought for a couple of minutes before he spoke. "I want to be a part of what you plan to do here, but I don't want to be an owner, if that's what you're asking."

"Why not?"

"This is what Kade wanted for you. That's what he wanted for me." Brodie looked over to where Alex and Peyton were getting out of Alex's car. "He gave her to me because she's what I needed. I guess he gave me to her, too."

Both Maddox and Naught nodded their heads.

Last night he hadn't been sure he could set foot on this land again, but when they drove up earlier, something inside of him told him he belonged here.

Whatever Kade had done in his life to be able to give this land to him and Naught wasn't as important as why he had. He did it to fulfill his brothers' dream.

"If there's nothin' else, I've got guys workin' the fields." When Maddox shook his head, Naughton walked into the woods.

"Where's he going?" Alex asked.

"The north vineyards," he answered, realizing this was her first time here. "I can't wait to show it all to you."

"Hey, Mad, unless you need my help with something here, I'm gonna get Peyton out of this heat."

"No, go ahead, Brodie. Just let me know if you have any questions about what we discussed."

"Do the parents know?"

"Not yet. That's something we'll have to talk about. We need to tell Skye and Ainsley too."

Alex hugged Peyton, and then kissed Maddox's cheek when Brodie and Peyton walked away.

"You missed," he said, turning to cover her lips with his.

"Go get in the truck, and I'll try again."

As screwed up as everything was, just having Alex with him today made it manageable.

Maddox climbed in the driver's side, leaned over, and put his arm around her shoulders. "Thanks, Al."

She pulled him close, spun around, and sat on his lap. "You can do better than that, Mad-man. Kiss me like you mean it."

"Gladly." Maddox didn't hesitate. At the same time his tongue found hers, his hand crept under her shirt and teased her nipple. "I gotta get you out of these clothes."

"Everyone gone?"

Maddox looked around, and when he didn't see any sign of his brothers or Peyton, he didn't waste any time getting her shirt and bra off. He flung them over the seat, and feasted on her breasts. "Too damn long since I had a taste of you."

"What, an hour?" She laughed, slid off his lap, and pulled at his belt. "Me, too, Mad. Get these pants off."

"Goddamn, Alex. What you do to me, girl."

Maddox closed his eyes and concentrated on the amazing things Alex could do when she took him in her mouth. This was another thing he'd taught her, and she'd learned well. It didn't take long before he felt himself on the edge.

"Let yourself go, Mad. Quit thinkin'."

As soon as she put her mouth back where it had been, he did what he was told.

—:—

Alex looked around for her shirt and bra.

"It's behind the seat, darlin'."

She turned to reach over the seat, but he stopped her.

"I'll get it." Maddox could reach her clothes almost without trying.

"*Shit!*" Alex hunched down on the front seat.

"What?" Maddox turned his head and saw why she had screamed. Her brother Gabe was pulling up behind them.

"Shit, shit, shit," she said again.

"Can I do anything to help?"

"Got anywhere I can hide?"

If Gabe found her half-naked in the front of Mad's truck, she'd never hear the end of it.

Alex was dressed before Gabe got out of his truck, but it hadn't been a moment too soon. He stormed toward them as Maddox opened the door and got out.

"Hey, Gabe—"

Before Maddox could finish, Gabe had him by the throat and knocked up against the truck.

"*Gabe!*" Alex screamed. "*What the hell?*" She opened the door and ran around to the other side of the vehicle. "*Let him go! What are you doing?*"

"*Where is that no-good, fucking brother of yours?*"

Maddox pried Gabe's fingers from his throat and pushed him back. Gabe came back swinging, and Alex jumped in front of Maddox.

"*Jesus Fucking Christ!*" Alex heard Mad yell as she hit the ground.

Instead of hitting Maddox, Gabe's fist had landed squarely in her abdomen. She struggled to catch her breath, but the pain in her stomach was so severe, she thought she might pass out.

"*You stupid, fucking asshole,*" Maddox yelled at Gabe. "*She just had surgery.*"

Mad's arms went around her, and he picked her up. He gently laid her on the back seat of her car, while Alex slipped in and out of awareness.

"Go around and get in. You'll have to hold her while I drive," Maddox yelled at Gabe.

It was the last thing she heard.

20

"Are you immediate family?" the nurse in the emergency room asked.

"Emma, it's me, Maddox Butler. *You've known me your whole life.*"

"Don't yell at me, Maddox. I'm supposed to ask."

"He is." Maddox slammed his finger in Gabe's chest.

"Can you sign this, please?" Emma handed Gabe a clipboard and showed him where to sign.

"How is she?" Maddox asked.

"The doctor is with her right now. I'll let you know as soon as I hear anything."

When Emma went back through the emergency room doors, Maddox turned away from Gabe and went outside.

Neither spoke on the way to the hospital, and hadn't said anything directly to each other since they'd arrived. If Gabe approached him, Maddox wasn't sure what he'd do. It was safer to keep his distance. One Avila in the hospital was enough for today.

He heard the automatic door open and could sense Gabe standing behind him.

"Don't say a word, Gabe. I'm warning you. I came out here for a reason. You get an inch closer to me, and I swear I'll kill you."

"Alex has internal bleeding. They're taking her straight into surgery."

"If anything…" Maddox couldn't continue.

He was sitting in the waiting room when Peyton came in followed by Brodie and Naughton.

"What happened?" Peyton asked.

"How—"

"Gabe called Lucia, who called my mom," Peyton explained. "All she said was that Alex was in surgery."

"There was an accident," Maddox began. He couldn't remember the last time he saw Gabe, but if the *sonuvabitch* left the hospital while his sister was still in surgery, it would just give him another reason to kill him.

"Maddox?" Brodie put his hand on Maddox's shoulder.

"We'll talk about it later. Okay?"

"Okay. Whatever you want to do."

"You see Gabe Avila anywhere?" Maddox looked at the three of them who all shook their heads.

"He showed up at Demetria wanting to know where my brother was. I'm paraphrasing, given I'd rather not repeat the string of curse words that prefaced 'my brother.'"

"Demetria?"

"The property on Old Creek Road."

Brodie nodded his head.

"Another subject for later. Okay, Brodie?"

"Whatever, Mad. You don't have to explain anything right now."

"I can't think about anything other than Alex right now."

"I get it. Have they said anything about how the surgery is going?"

Peyton's phone pinged a few minutes later. "My mom texted that she's with Lucia and Gabe in the surgical waiting room. She'll let me know as soon as they hear how Alex is."

An hour later, Peyton's mother walked in with Lucia. Maddox stood, and Lucia put her arms around him.

"Alex is going to be fine. She's in recovery now, but she'll be moved to a room within the hour. She's asking for you, *mijo*."

"When can I see her?"

"The nurse said she'd call down here as soon as Alex was moved."

"Thanks, Mrs. Wolf."

She brought her hand to his cheek. "Dear, Maddox. Please, call me August."

"Yes, ma'am."

Peyton, her mom, and Lucia laughed.

"Sorcha raised you to be a gentleman. My Alex is a very lucky woman to have you in her life, Maddox."

"Thank you, Lucia."

Lucia put her hand on his cheek, like August had. "Dear Maddox," she teased. "Please, call me Mama."

When he smiled, so did everyone else. It was a nice moment in a few days of what felt like a bad dream. He only hoped Gabe wasn't around the corner. Seeing him would turn his bad dream into Gabe's nightmare.

"Hi, Emma," said Peyton. "I didn't know you worked here."

"I've been here about six months. It's a nice hospital. Sometimes it's difficult since I know so many people who come in. They make it hard for me to fol-low the rules." She looked at Maddox, who shrugged.

"You can see her now. She's in room four-twelve. Take the elevator and turn—"

Maddox was on his way to the elevator before Emma finished. He knew where to go.

—:—

Alex tried to roll to her side, but it hurt too much. She closed her eyes and rested back against the bed. She must've drifted off, but the sound of the door open-ing woke her. Instead of Maddox, Gabe walked in.

"Get out, Gabe."

"Alex, I—"

"Get out. I know it's hard for you to muster up any respect for me, but maybe just this once, you could do what I ask and leave me the hell alone."

Alex turned her head and closed her eyes, praying Gabe would be gone before Maddox came upstairs.

—:—

"Hey, sweetheart." Maddox ran his fingers through her hair and kissed her forehead.

"Hi, Mad. I'm so glad you're here."

"Where else would I be?"

"Keep me awake, would you? I've been having some weird-ass dreams."

"Yeah? About what?"

"Kade."

"Talkin' to you?"

Alex nodded.

"What did he say?"

"He told me to leave things alone."

Maddox scratched his beard, and Alex's eyes focused on his hands.

"Think I should shave it off?"

"No, I like it."

"What else did Kade say?"

"That was it. One sentence. *Leave things alone.* Damn anesthesia. Just when I was getting it out of my system, now I have to start all over."

"I'm sorry."

"You don't have anything to be sorry for."

"I wish I knew what was going on between your family and mine. I'd ask Gabe, but if I saw him right now, I'm afraid of what I might do to him."

"He was here a few minutes ago, but I threw him out."

Maddox wasn't sure what to say. He was glad she had, but he was her brother, and there was something going on that had made him throw that punch. It was meant for him, not Alex. If she hadn't jumped between them, she wouldn't be in this hospital bed.

He was still too angry to seek Gabe out, but soon he would, and then he'd get to the bottom of why Gabe was so mad in the first place.

"What are you thinking about?"

"Nothing."

"Liar. Come closer."

When he did, Alex ran her fingers over his forehead. "Your brow is furrowed."

"Yeah? I guess it's because I'm worried about you."

"No big deal. Gabe's punch just landed in the exact right place to rupture the internal surgical site."

"How bad was it?"

"Not bad, they fixed it laparoscopically. Look." Alex moved the gown away from her abdomen and showed Maddox three small incisions.

"You can hardly see them."

"I don't have to start over with the healing process. I swear I'd kill Gabe if I had to do that."

He knew she didn't mean it the way he was feeling it. He'd never felt the kind of rage he did when Alex had crumpled to the ground after Gabe hit her. He never thought he could kill another human being, but in that moment, he knew he could've, and it scared the shit out of him.

"Did anyone say how long you have to be in here?"

"I can go home tomorrow if things go okay."

"That's great," he murmured.

"You're distracted."

"Hard not to be. There's a reason Gabe came looking for one of my brothers, and I need to find out what it is."

"He's such an asshole. I can't remember much about what happened. What did he say?"

"I believe his exact words were, 'where is that no-good, fucking brother of yours?'"

"Do you think he meant Naughton?"

"Both Brodie and Naughton were at Demetria. I can't figure out what he'd want with either, though."

"How'd you come up with the name?"

Maddox explained that the land had originally belonged to Lena's mother's parents, and that was what the estate was called then. It was only after her mother married Fred Hess that people started calling it the Hess estate.

"I like it."

"Yeah, as soon as Naught and I heard it, we knew. We didn't even have to talk about it. We just knew. Now I'm not sure. All the shit with Kade and Lena…"

"Forget about Kade and Lena. It's in the past. It's a good name, and it feels right. That's all that matters."

"You're right, I guess."

"You guess. Will you ever learn, Mad?" She smiled and so did he. "Tell me about it."

"From what we've seen so far, Lena's grandparents had a very advanced operation at one time. She said her grandfather suffered from Parkinson's, and after he died, her mother didn't want to live in the house."

"What house?"

"I keep forgetting you haven't really been there." Maddox shook his head.

"What does that mean?"

"Every step I took, I imagined you being there with me. That's why I keep forgetting you weren't. There's so much I want to show you. The house is just one of many amazing things I've discovered."

"Tell me more."

Maddox described it as he had seen it, one discovery after another. The vineyards, the views, the caves, and finally the winery and house on the hilltop. He left out the part about the barrels of wine he and Naughton had discovered, that evidently weren't there any longer.

"What did Naught mean when he said the wine was gone?"

"It's like you can read my mind. I was just thinking about that. When we were exploring the caves, we found a locked room full of barrels of wine. I only tasted from one, but I think it was all Cabernet Sauvignon. At first I thought it was wine left there from years ago, but once Naught shone light on them, it was evident the barrels were new, confirming the wine I tasted wasn't very old."

Alex closed her eyes, and worry marked her forehead the way it had his. "Who do you think it belongs to?"

Maddox shrugged.

"The bond."

"It's only one theory, Al."

"Tell me more about the house."

"It isn't in bad shape, considering it's sat empty for twenty-odd years. Needs a floor to ceiling cleaning, but otherwise, I think it might be inhabitable."

"Will you live there?"

"I'm not sure. It depends."

"On what?"

"How well you like it." From the moment he set foot inside, he'd envisioned Alex living there with him. He hadn't even seen the whole house. He didn't make it upstairs after the heartache episode.

"What does Naught think of it?"

"I haven't asked. Naughton is never forthcoming with much information when you do ask, let alone when you don't."

"Ask him."

"I will."

"Will you take me there?"

"Sure. As soon as you're up to it."

"Tomorrow."

Maddox smiled. Alex's eyes were drifting closed. Soon she'd be asleep, and he could stare at her all he wanted. She was a beautiful girl who'd matured into a stunning woman. She was smart, and funny, and definitely kept him on his toes. To think he'd almost lost her because of his own stupid pride.

"What are you thinking about now?" she murmured.

"Why, do I look worried?"

"No, you look happy."

Maddox leaned forward and kissed her. "I was thinking about how much I love you."

"Mmm. I like that. I love you too, Maddox."

Crazy to think that, in all those years, they never told each other how they felt, and yet now, the words were so easy to say.

"I'm gonna sleep for a little bit."

"Go right ahead. I'll go down and grab some food, but I'll be right back."

Alex's eyes were closed, but she nodded and smiled.

"Can I see her?" Peyton asked when Maddox walked back into the waiting room.

"Of course you can, but she might be asleep."

"Maybe we should come back later," she said to Brodie. "Lucia will want to see her, and…"

"Go up and see her now," Maddox told her. "She may not be talkative, but she'll be disappointed when she wakes up later to hear you were here but she didn't get the chance to talk to you."

"If you're sure."

"Peyton, I'm not Alex's gatekeeper. Go." He nudged her with his shoulder, and she smiled.

—:—

"There he is." Alex was sitting up in bed when Maddox came back upstairs later.

"Have you slept at all?"

"Peyton was here, and then they brought food." Alex ran her hand over her tray. "Not particularly appetizing food, but sustenance at least."

"Want me to go get you something better?"

"No, I don't want you to leave. You could send someone, though."

He smiled, not just with his mouth, but through his eyes too.

"What would you like?"

Alex raised her eyebrows.

"Pizza?"

"You got it, Mad-man. I guess I better ask first if I can have it."

Alex pressed the button on the call box and studied Maddox. He held on to so much tension, she could see it on his face and in his shoulders. His arm twitched, as though he fought the reflex to rub the back of his neck.

"How was your visit with Peyton?"

"Good. I feel like crap about Stave, though. I feel like I've abandoned it completely. That's what we talked about most."

"That you've abandoned Stave?"

"No, and yes. But not in a bad way. She asked if I'd agree to offering Sam a full-time job."

"Would you?"

"Of course. We've talked about it before, but then we decided it was silly since, between the two of us, we had a lot of flexibility. Now that she's pregnant, she and Brodie are looking for a place to live…"

"Does Sam want the job?"

"Definitely. In fact, I think it was Sam's idea. She's been putting in so many hours, she might've been looking for a raise."

"That's great, Al."

"Maddox?"

"Yeah?"

"It's silly to ask you what you're thinking about, I mean, there's so much, but what, right this minute?"

"I want to meet with the attorney. Naught says he doesn't know anything, but still."

"Have you tried to reach Lena?"

"I did earlier, when I went downstairs."

"And?"

"The number's no longer valid."

"Why would she disconnect her number?"

"Good question. She told me she was leaving yesterday, which I didn't think was a big deal."

"You found out she was married to Kade, but now that you know, what reason would there be for her to leave?"

"Right."

"You think there's something else she's hiding."

"I have no idea what, though."

"So, about that pizza?"

"Yeah, where is that nurse?"

"Can you see if you can find her?"

Maddox nodded and left the room. Alex grabbed her cell and texted Gabe.

You want me to forgive you, tell me why you were looking for Naughton.

Alex watched the three dots on her phone, waiting to see what Gabe's response was.

When?

It took him that long to text one word?

Later tonight.

Maddox came back in the room. "You're approved for junk food. Naught's on his way to get your favorites."

"All of them?"

"You got it."

"Do you know all my favorites, Mad?"

He raised an eyebrow and smiled. "He's gonna pick up some stuff for me and get the pizza on the way back. Can you wait forty-five minutes, or do you want me to go downstairs and get something to tide you over?"

"I'm pretty hungry. What's he getting for you?"

"Clothes, my toothbrush. That kind of stuff."

"Why?"

"Why do you think?"

"You're staying here tonight?"

"Sure am. Nurse Lucy is arranging for a cot for me now."

"You're kidding."

Maddox shook his head and sat on the side of the bed. "You're gonna have a damn hard time gettin' rid of me now, Alex."

Shit. Now what? She wouldn't be able to talk to Gabe with Maddox here.

"You don't look happy."

Alex thought a lot about what she wanted to say before she said it, and Maddox uncharacteristically waited patiently.

"I'm used to us going our separate ways pretty much all the time."

Maddox didn't say anything, so she kept talking.

"It isn't as though I don't believe you'll stick around, it's just that it's always been my decision."

He smiled.

"And you've done a good job letting me come and go."

Maddox nodded.

"When I didn't look happy, it was because I texted Gabe earlier and told him he needed to tell me why he was looking for Naughton this morning."

"If I'm here, he can't do that. Or won't."

"He sure wanted you to listen to him this morning, enough to pound on you."

"What's the problem, then?"

"You don't want to see him."

"Got it. So you're thinking for me."

Alex nodded.

"You're used to having to, but you don't anymore."

"Okay."

"See how easy that was? I noticed you were unhappy. You told me why; now we can work out a solution."

"Think that means we're grownups?"

"We're gettin' there. What did you tell Gabe?"

Alex showed him the text.

"Text him again and tell him to come now."

"Where will you be?"

He winked. "Right here, Al, by your side. Why can't you remember that?"

"Okay, I guess a hospital is the best place for you to be if you're gonna try to kill each other."

—:—

Maddox had no intention of hurting Gabe. The longer he talked to Alex, and felt her next to him, the less angry he was at her brother. Gabe hadn't meant to hurt Alex, and he must've had a good reason for taking a swing at him.

Naughton came in, a half hour later, carrying a pizza box, a paper bag, and a few other carryout boxes.

"Whatcha got there?"

"You said she wanted pizza and a bunch of other junk food." Naughton set the boxes and bag on the ledge by the window. "Wings, garlic bread, dipping sauce, candy, cookies, and soda."

"Did you get my stuff?"

"Still in the truck."

"I'll walk you out."

"Guess I'm leaving. Bye, Alex."

"Bye, Naughton. Thanks for the food."

Maddox leaned over and kissed her forehead. "Be right back."

"You two are lookin' more like Peyton and Brodie today," Naught said while they waited for the elevator.

"I'm gonna try."

"To do what?"

"Get her to marry me."

Naughton didn't say anything else until they got to the truck.

"Thanks for bringing Al's food and for picking up my stuff."

"No problem." Naughton handed Maddox his bag, climbed in the truck, closed the door, and started the engine.

Maddox backed away and watched his brother drive off.

Did Gabe think Naughton was somehow mixed up in Los Cab's bond issue? And if he did, why?

There was no reason for Naught to care what kind of business the Avila's winery did. What was good for them was good for everyone else in the collaborative.

The feud between the two families ended over five years ago, and it hadn't been Naught's feud; it was between their father and Alfonso Avila.

His involvement made no sense. Naughton was a live and let live kind of guy. He wouldn't have the time or interest to interfere in anyone else's business.

The missing wine barrels were a clue, though. Did the wine belong to Los Cab, and if it did, had Gabe come looking for it this morning?

Something else was bothering him. Maddox looked back through his texts from Naughton and noticed his brother had texted him before seven this morning.

How had Naughton managed to get the labor crew started, find out Lena had left and her house was empty, and gone to the caves to find the wine was missing between the time he left Butler Ranch and the time he sent the text?

<h1 style="text-align:center">21</h1>

"Hear anything from Gabe?"

"I'm surprised you didn't see him on your way up. He should be here any minute."

"Any food left?"

Alex stuck her tongue out at him.

"Don't offer somethin' you aren't capable of delivering, Al."

Maddox opened the pizza box. "You haven't had any."

"Uh, not supposed to get out of bed on my own."

"I'm sorry. I didn't realize…"

"You should be sorry. Here I am, starving to death, and you don't even think of giving me a piece of pizza before you leave."

She might be teasing now, but there was a time he wouldn't have given her or her hunger a second thought.

"Knock, knock." Gabe stood in the doorway, hands in his pockets.

"Hi, Gabe." Maddox walked over and reached out to shake hands.

"If I were you I'd take a swing at me, not shake my hand."

"Yeah, well, you weren't lookin' for me this morning, and you sure as hell didn't mean to hit your sister."

Gabe shook Maddox's hand and walked over to Alex.

"I owe you more than one apology, Alex."

"You sure do. Hug me, Gabe, and tell me how sorry you are."

Maddox watched Gabe lean down and gently hug his sister. Alex closed her eyes, but he knew she was crying.

"All that stuff I said, I was wrong. I've been stressed to the max, and none of it was your fault."

"Why didn't you just tell me the truth, Gabe?"

Gabe looked at Maddox. "Because I thought you'd tell him."

"Tell us both, and let's see if we can get to the bottom of what's going on."

"You sure you want to do this?" Gabe looked at Alex and then back at Maddox.

"No one expects you to handle everything on your own, Gabe."

He pointed at the chair near Alex's bed. "Mind if I sit? Haven't been sleeping very well."

Alex nodded at her brother and motioned for him to move closer.

"Start at the beginning if you can."

Gabe leaned forward in the chair and put his elbows on his knees.

"Enzo came to me about six months ago, saying he thought it was time for him to work someplace other than Los Cab. He had a lot of reasons why he wanted to leave, most of which had to do with me and the way he said I treat him.

"I only half-listened to him. And when he was done talking, I told him he was crazy to leave a good job with his own family's winery, and that I doubted he'd find anything else that would pay half as much."

Gabe sat up and looked between Maddox and Alex again. "Asshole, right?"

Alex nodded, but smiled. "Go on, Gabe."

"Things went downhill from there. Enzo was pissed at me, and I was pissed right back at him. We only argued. We never talked."

Maddox watched Gabe as he talked. He was agitated, but contrite. He was the oldest son in a proud

Hispanic family. Admitting to Alex that he'd mishandled things with Enzo had to be very difficult.

"It got to the point where if I was in the winery, he'd turn around and walk out. If I came in and he was there, he'd leave. We communicated through Trev or Mama, if at all."

Gabe stood and walked over to the window. "That's when things at the winery started falling apart. I didn't realize it at the time, but in hindsight…"

"I saw you two a couple weeks ago. Things didn't seem strained then."

"Think back, Alex. It was."

He was right. Enzo had offered to go for a ride with her, and Gabe gave him the stink eye.

"I may have been able to help Enzo sort things out three months ago, when he realized there was a problem, but he was afraid to come to me."

"Two days ago, you said he was overreacting."

"That's because I didn't know the extent of the problem until this morning."

"What happened this morning?"

"We were raided by the Alcohol Tax Bureau."

"What did they find?" Maddox asked.

"A lot more wine than I knew was there."

"How is this possible, Gabe? You weren't aware of how much wine you were making?"

"I wasn't aware of how much wine we were storing. There's a big difference, Alex."

"He's right," Maddox added. "Big difference. I don't monitor it at Butler Ranch, Brodie does. He handles compliance."

"What did you do when Brodie was gone?" she asked.

"I took over then, but if you aren't the one doing it day in, day out, it's hard to manage along with everything else."

"Who were you looking for this morning?" Alex asked Gabe.

"I'll get to that, but I want to backtrack a little."

Alex nodded.

"Enzo came to me two days ago, the same morning he visited you, and told me he'd been storing unmarked barrels in the caves on the Hess Estate. He heard about Kade leaving you the property, and was there the day you and Naughton discovered the barrels."

"That's when he panicked."

"That's right. He knew one of two things were going to happen. He'd either lose access to the caves, and thus lose the wine, or you'd start asking questions about who it belonged to."

"Lena Hess knew."

"Enzo said she caught him there a few weeks ago. He promised he'd get the wine out of the caves, that he just needed a little time to rework the numbers and get into compliance.

"That day, when you and Naughton were in the caves, Enzo said he heard Naughton say he figured the wine belonged to someone with a bond issue."

"It was one theory."

"Logical one."

"You think Naughton set this up."

"Someone hauled the wine to Los Cab. The same person called the ATB. Someone wants us to lose our bond."

Maddox would argue that Naughton wouldn't have any reason to care, or the time to move the wine, but he still had questions only his brother could answer.

"Butler Ranch has no quarrel with Los Caballeros," Maddox said confidently. "Even when our families feuded, I know in my heart, my father never would've done anything to jeopardize your bond or your business.

The feud between our fathers was a matter of pride. It wasn't about hatred or even competition."

"I agree, Gabe," Alex spoke. "Papa and Laird could've been friends if it weren't for that stupid Zin medal."

Through the years, Maddox had thought a lot about what Alex just said. It was a shame the two men hadn't reconciled before Alfonso's death.

"How bad is it?" Alex asked.

"I won't know for several days. We're facing fines and penalties for sure. It may get as bad as suspension or revocation."

"Why do you think it was Naughton who moved the wine and contacted the ATB?"

"There was a witness."

"Who?" Alex gasped.

"Rory Calder."

Alex grimaced. "Tell us what he told you."

"He showed up not long after the ATB arrived. Said that there'd been rumors about our bond and about us storing wine in the caves on the Hess Estate. That's when Enzo told us about overhearing you and Naughton that day. Rory said he saw Naughton moving the barrels."

"Did he have proof?" Maddox asked.

"With everything happening, I took him at his word."

"Gabe," Alex began. "How well do you know Rory Calder?"

"Not well. Just met him this morning, but I heard Calder Wines bought Tablas Creek a few weeks ago. Why?"

Alex and Maddox told Gabe about their individual run-ins with Rory.

"You think he's the one behind this?" Gabe asked.

"I had dinner with Noah Ridge, a couple nights ago, and he mentioned that if we ever wanted to sell Los Cab, there'd be a number of interested parties. I can't remember his exact words, but he gave me the impression Calder Wines would be a bidder."

"Why would we sell?"

"Exactly, Gabe."

"You believe Calder somehow found out Enzo was storing wine at Hess, and orchestrated this whole thing."

"We'd have to ask Lena, or the agent representing Hess when they had the remaining land on the market, but my guess is Calder was a potential buyer."

"When was it on the market?" Maddox asked Alex.

"I'm not sure, but not very long ago. Ridge Winery was definitely interested; Noah said he toured the property before they made an offer."

"What else did *Noah* tell you?" Maddox asked, not trying very hard to hide his sneer.

Alex rolled her eyes. "A couple things I found interesting. First, that 'the family' took it off the market. Second, that anyone interested in looking at it had to sign a non-disclosure agreement before they were permitted access."

"Why?"

"He didn't say. He only said that he told me more than he should've."

"Back up a minute," said Gabe. "Tell me about Lena's involvement."

Maddox looked at Alex, who shook her head.

"I don't think she played a significant role, but she'd know who looked at the property." Maddox thought for a minute. "If we're able to reach Lena and she tells us Calder was behind moving the wine and calling the ATB, we'd still have to prove it. Even if we did all that, it wouldn't help your bond issue. All it would do is tell us who was behind turning you in."

Gabe nodded. "I'd still like to know."

"Me, too," mumbled Maddox, who caught a glimpse of Alex grimacing. "What's wrong?"

"Pain meds are wearing off."

"Do you want me to call the nurse?"

"Yeah, I think you better."

"Hey, Gabe, would you take a walk with me?"

Gabe nodded.

"We'll be right back, Al." Maddox leaned down and kissed her forehead. "Whoa, you're burnin' up."

"Yeah, I don't feel so good."

Gabe followed Maddox to the nurses' station. "Listen, I want to talk to you, but Alex—"

"Can I help you?" a nurse asked.

"Alex Avila, in room four-twelve. She said she's in some pain. She's also burning up."

"I was just on my way to check her vitals."

Maddox and Gabe followed her, but when they got to the room, the nurse asked them to wait outside.

"As long as we have a minute alone, I want you to know, whatever Butler Ranch can do to help, we will."

"I appreciate the offer. I'm not entirely sure what to expect."

Maddox wouldn't know what to expect either. They'd never had a bond issue, and couldn't imagine being in Gabe's shoes.

"Have you given any thought to what you'll do?"

"I've played out every scenario, including revocation. I don't believe it'll go that far. We've never been out of compliance before, and we've been making wine for decades. There has to be some leeway for a first-time offender."

Maddox nodded his head. He agreed. "If necessary, I'd be willing to underwrite your bond."

"What did you just say?"

"You heard me."

"You'd do that, Maddox?"

"Yes, I would."

"You know how much money we're talking?"

"Very well aware."

"Why?"

"As I told someone the other night—as a matter of fact, it was Rory Calder. Anyway, what I said was, when a member of the collaborative is in trouble, we come together to help privately, not publicly. I know once word gets out to the other members, mine won't be the only offer of help."

"There's more to it, isn't there?"

"What do you mean?"

"What's going on with you and Alex?"

"My offer to help would've come whether Alex and I were together or not. However, since I hope one day soon we'll be family, I'm extending it now. Whatever you need, Gabe."

"Maddox, I don't know what to say. You're a good man, just like your father."

The nurse opened the door to Alex's room. "She's okay. You can go back in."

"What about the fever?" asked Maddox.

"She's warm, but only a couple degrees above normal. It's to be expected, but we'll keep an eye on her through the night."

"I'll be here too."

The nurse looked Maddox up and down and fanned her face. "Lucy told us about you."

"Stay away from him; he's mine," Alex shouted. "By the way, would someone mind getting me another piece of *my* pizza?"

"See? She's gonna be fine." The nurse patted Maddox's arm and walked away.

Maddox got Alex's plate and gave her the biggest slice of the pie. "Gabe, would you like some pizza, or any other junk food known to man?"

"You know, I was about to decline, but I don't remember when I last ate, and for the first time in a long while, I'm hungry."

Maddox dished two slices for Gabe and one for himself.

"Uh, anywhere I can use a restroom, and maybe get some coffee?"

"Down the hall, to the left, you can find both," Maddox told him.

Maddox bent over to kiss Alex once Gabe left, and she put her palm on his cheek.

"Thank you."

"For what?"

"Making Gabe feel better."

Had he? He wasn't sure. Los Caballeros still faced a tough battle, and the outcome was hard to predict.

"What else are you worried about?" she asked.

Lena's sudden departure weighed heavy on his mind. He couldn't help but wonder if Los Cab's bond, the wine hidden in the caves, and the ATB had anything to do with it. There was also the question of Naughton's odd behavior. Did the three relate somehow?

Maddox's phone pinged.

"What is it?"

"A text from Lena, but from an unknown number, asking if I can meet her tonight." Maddox looked up at Alex.

"You're kidding?"

"Nope."

"What?" Gabe asked, coming back in with his coffee. "You two look like you've seen a ghost."

"More like a devil," Alex muttered.

"Huh?" her brother asked.

"You know the expression 'speak of the devil'? The devil just spoke."

Gabe looked at Maddox. "What's she talking about?"

"I just got a text from Lena Hess, asking if I could meet her tonight."

"What are you going to do?" asked Alex.

Maddox shrugged.

"If you're worried about me, you don't need to be. I'm in a hospital. If anything goes wrong, there are plenty of people to take care of me."

"It isn't just that."

"What else?"

"It's gonna sound crazy."

"Just tell us, Mad."

"I don't have a good feeling about this."

"I can go with you," offered Gabe.

"What do you think, Al?"

"Trust your instincts. If something doesn't feel right, either don't go, or don't go alone. Did she say where she wanted to meet?"

"At the house."

"Whose house?"

"The one on the hilltop."

"Don't you mean *our* house?" Alex smiled.

22

"You sure you don't mind going along?" Maddox asked Gabe on their way to the parking structure.

Gabe took so long to answer, Maddox was beginning to think he hadn't heard him.

"I want to go with you, for a lot of reasons."

"Yeah?"

"Maybe Lena knows who really moved the wine from the caves and brought the barrels to Los Cab. But that isn't all."

"I can drive, unless you want to meet there," Maddox offered when they got to his truck.

"Nah, I'm good. I only live a couple blocks from here, and if you're coming back…"

"I am." Maddox unlocked the doors.

They'd been on the road a couple of minutes when Maddox asked Gabe his other reasons for wanting to go along. "I'm just curious," Maddox added.

They were almost to the highway when Gabe finally spoke.

"Your family has done so much for our family. We can never repay your kindness. You and your father saved us after my father died. And now? Less than half an hour ago, you offered to underwrite our bond. I hope it doesn't come to that, but I know that if it does, you're a man of your word, and you wouldn't make the offer if you didn't intend to follow through."

"You're right about that. If you need help, I'll help."

"Why do you think Lena wants to meet you?"

Maddox scrubbed over his face with his hand. "It's really complicated, but…shit…"

Gabe held up a hand. "If it's none of my business…"

"It isn't that. It's just…Lena is Kade's ex-wife."

"What?"

"I know. I only found out yesterday."

"I thought her last name was Hess."

"Yeah, don't know about that. Guess she changed it back, or never changed it to Butler in the first place. Obviously their marriage was a secret."

"Why?"

"Like I said, I only found out about it yesterday."

Gabe shook his head. "Wow."

"I know. Uh, listen, you need to keep this quiet for a bit. My brothers and I haven't had a chance to talk to our parents or sisters yet."

"No problem. I get it." Gabe laughed.

"What's funny?"

"Sorry. This is big. I get that. I just laughed because I never get around to telling my family much of anything. I'm sure I drive them crazy. Our father was the same way."

"I hear that."

"I think I'm doing the right thing by handling everything, but then it comes back to bite me in the ass."

"I told Alex that I struggle with being the oldest brother, and she suggested that my siblings might not want me to feel as though I have to step into any perceived role."

"Like I have?"

"I always believed Kade took care of us in his own way, or maybe that's just what we wanted to think. He was certainly there for me when I needed to run stuff by him, but if I believed he felt pressured to carry the burden of our family's problems, I never would've let him."

"What was Alex's advice?"

"To talk to my brothers and sisters, and tell them how I was feeling."

"How's that going for you?"

"Haven't tried it out yet."

"Think you will?"

"Not a chance in hell."

"This place is amazing," Gabe said, getting out of the truck.

Maddox pointed out the three buildings. "That was the main winery. The one next to it was left unfinished, but Naughton and I think it was meant to be a tasting room. The far building is the house. That's where we're meeting Lena."

"Is she here?"

"I don't think so. I didn't see her car when we drove by the house near the front gate, and it isn't here."

Maddox opened the door to the winery building and let Gabe stick his head in. "I'll show you when it's daylight."

Gabe nodded and followed Maddox to the house.

"All of it is pretty incredible, but this is far and away the best part."

Maddox opened the massive door and walked into the foyer. "It'll be dark soon, and I've never been in here at night. I'm not even sure if there's electricity."

"There is." Lena came around the corner from the kitchen and hit a switch that illuminated the entire space.

"*Jesus,* you scared the crap out of me."

"Sorry. I didn't want anyone to know I was here. Who's this?" Lena approached Gabe.

"Gabe Avila, Alex's brother. He runs Los Cab."

"I see."

"I can wait in the truck," Gabe offered.

"No, this concerns you too, so you might as well stay."

"What's goin' on Lena?"

"We should sit." She walked back into the kitchen, switching on lights as they went. "It's pretty difficult to see this side of the house, but I closed the drapes anyway."

"Who are you hiding from?"

She poured a glass of wine from a bottle sitting on the table. "Help yourselves," she said before she took a swig from her glass. "You were right when you suspected I knew who put the wine in the caves. I knew it was Enzo, and I knew why."

"Did you—"

Lena held up her hand. "Before you ask, no, I didn't call the ATB. I told Enzo he could store the wine in the caves as long as he needed to. It only became a problem when I put the other two hundred hectares up for sale."

She looked up at Maddox. "I took it off the market before Peter contacted your parents."

Maddox nodded. "So what happened?"

"The caves weren't on land that was for sale, and no one should've been in them."

"But someone was."

"Yes. Rory Calder was."

"Doesn't surprise me. What did he do?"

Lena took a deep breath. "The agent who listed the property had specific instructions. Everyone who looked at it had to sign a non-disclosure agreement. Most of those who did, didn't care enough to ask the reason they were signing it. Most assumed it was because we wanted the details of the sale kept private, but that wasn't why."

"You didn't want anyone to know."

"Only someone who had an ulterior motive for digging deeper would've discovered Kade had owned the adjacent property and had deeded it to you and Naughton. After that, it wouldn't be that hard to find the marriage records."

Lena took another swig of wine. "Rory blackmailed me."

"How?"

She looked at Gabe, but Maddox nodded.

"Making my marriage to Kade public."

"Okay, but—"

"He wanted access to the caves, and wanted to know who the wine belonged to. I told him I didn't know, but he knew I was lying." She looked over at Gabe again. "He offered the vineyard guys Naught hired a lot of money to move the barrels last night."

Then Lena looked at Maddox. "He showed up not long after you left, wanting to know what you knew. I told him you didn't know anything, but he didn't believe me. He had to get back to the guys, but he told me he'd come back, and we'd 'talk.'"

"So you left."

"I had everything ready to go anyway. I sensed Rory planned to act."

"Naughton said your place was empty."

"I hired my own guys. It took a little over an hour to get everything out of the house and for me to be on my way."

"Where are you going?" Gabe asked her.

"I don't know yet."

Maddox had been watching the exchange between Gabe and Lena. Lena knew exactly where she was going, and she had no intention of telling them. He wouldn't ask now, not in front of Gabe, but he'd bet there was something else she was hiding. Now that the secret was out about her marriage to Kade, there was no reason for her to run, unless that wasn't what was really behind the blackmail.

"You're leaving tonight?"

She nodded.

Maddox pulled a card out of his wallet and a pen out of his jacket pocket. He wrote something on the back, folded it in half, and handed it to her.

"That's my cell, if you need anything, call me there."

She already had his cell, but she was smart enough not to unfold the card before she slipped it into her pocket. It confirmed there was more going on than what she'd told them. Lena was definitely hiding something else.

"Thank you." Lena stood. "You can contact our attorney if you decide you're interested in the rest of the land. For now, I don't plan to put it on the market."

"Who's your attorney?"

"Peter Wendt."

Maddox nodded. Made sense.

"Bye Maddox, and you too, Gabe."

Lena walked over to the staircase that led down to the basement, and waved.

"Where's she going?" Gabe asked.

"Through the caves," Maddox answered.

"What'd you write on the back of the card?" Gabe asked once they were back in the truck.

Maddox smiled. "Didn't miss that, huh?"

"She texted you earlier. Wouldn't take a genius."

"I wrote the time and place of our next meeting."

Gabe didn't ask when or where, and Maddox didn't offer.

"Kade was Delta Force," Gabe said.

"Yeah?"

"Think she's got a connection?"

Maddox hadn't thought of that, but it was a possibility. But then, why would she have let Rory blackmail her? Why wouldn't she call in help when she needed it?

When they got to the end of the one-lane road, Maddox's headlights caught something shiny parked way off in the woods near the creek.

"Shit."

"What?"

"I think that's Naught's truck."

"You don't need to worry about me—"

"I'm not. I'm worried about my brother."

Maddox parked and killed his engine. "Be right back."

"You want me to come with you?"

"Nah, I'm just gonna see if he's around."

Why was Naughton here? And where was he?

—:—

"Where's the truck?" Lena asked.

"Near the gate."

"Maddox just left. Alex's brother was with him."

"I parked far enough out of the way that he won't see it."

"I sure as hell hope you did. He's already asking too many questions." She pulled the card Maddox gave her out of her pocket.

"What's this?"

"Our next meeting."

"I'll handle it."

—:—

Maddox checked the truck and found it locked. Troubling, since they rarely locked their vehicles when they were on the ranch, in fact, they usually left the keys in them. Here or Butler Ranch wouldn't have made any difference. They were inside the gate.

He walked along the creek, but there was no sign of Naughton. Maybe he left the truck for the night and caught a ride back to Butler Ranch with one of the workers. That was the only logical explanation.

"Any sign of him?"

"Nope."

Where are you? Maddox texted.

Home, Naughton answered almost immediately.

Need to talk.

Where are you?

Leaving Demetria.

Coming straight back?

Damn, Maddox forgot he wasn't going home; he was staying at the hospital with Alex.

No, hospital, meet me there in an hour.

"You're back."

"Sorry I woke you. How are you feeling?"

"Better now that you're here. How'd it go?"

"Lena confirmed it was Calder who set up the ATB sting. I'm not sure there's anything that we can do about it though, at least from a legal standpoint. He didn't break any laws."

"He stole wine from the caves."

"And delivered it to its owners."

"What about illegally?" Alex smirked.

"Not sure about that either. Karma has a funny way of comin' around and bitin' you in the ass when you least expect it."

"By the way, what did you have on Lang to get him to drop the custody petition?"

"Once a cheater, always a cheater."

"What's that mean?"

"I don't predict the marriage to the new wife is gonna last any longer than Lang's marriage to Peyton did."

"You saw him?"

"Yep, but he didn't see me. Since it was after Brodie told us about the custody issue, I just happened to snap a couple photos."

Alex smiled. "Devious."

"Wily."

"Yep, you're like a coyote that way, aren't ya?"

"Did the trick. All that matters."

"What have you got in mind for Calder?"

"Don't know yet, but it wasn't that hard for us to piece together his involvement in the Los Cab bond issue. My guess is he's after land, and given how sloppy he was the last couple days, my prediction is it won't be long before he acts again."

"When's the next collaborative meeting?"

"Next month, but I think there's enough happening in the valley to call one sooner."

Maddox's phone pinged. Naughton was there, waiting for him downstairs.

"I'll be back soon. Try to get some sleep, and I'll try not to wake you up." He kissed her forehead again, relieved that it wasn't as warm as it had been earlier.

"You missed."

Maddox smiled and kissed her lips. Alex wound her arms around his neck and held him close.

"I wish this bed was big enough to fit both of us," she murmured.

"Follow the rules, and tomorrow night we'll sleep in one plenty big enough."

"Where are you going?"

"Naught's here. Couple things we need to talk about."

"Gonna give karma a little shove?"

"I don't know. Maybe."

"Hey." Maddox joined Naughton in the main lobby waiting area. "Thanks for meeting me here."

"What's up? You didn't ask me to bring you more clothes or food, so what do you need?"

"We need to talk, Naughton. I have a lot of questions, and I'm hoping you have a lot of answers."

Naughton nodded, and Maddox motioned for him to follow him outside.

"I don't know where to start," Maddox began once they found chairs outside.

"Heard about the ATB raid. Guess that explains why the wine was gone, and confirms who it belonged to."

"Yeah, about that. How'd you know it was gone, Naught?"

"I looked." Naughton shook his head at him, almost as though he thought Maddox was an idiot.

"I figured that much, but how'd you do it all so fast? You left Butler Ranch at dawn, got a crew started, discovered Lena and the wine were gone, all before seven."

Naughton stood. "Is there somethin' you're accusing me of, Maddox?"

"No, I'm just askin'." Maddox's eyes bored into his brother's, letting him know he wasn't giving up until he got an answer.

"I can't believe I'm doing this, but here goes. I left Butler Ranch a little after five. I arrived at the Old Creek Road gates, where the labor contractor was waiting with a crew, before five-thirty. I gave him a map and outlined where we'd start.

"I was about to get back in the truck to lead them to the vineyard when I noticed something off at Lena's. It looked like the front door was open, not good at five in the morning, so I told the guys I'd be right behind them. I walked over and knocked, but she didn't answer, so I stuck my head inside. That's how I knew the place was empty."

Maddox nodded his head. "Go on."

"You canceled dinner. She skipped town. It was all a little weird, so instead of meeting the guys, I went up to the house. As long as I was there, I thought I'd see if I could find the other entrance to the caves. That's when I discovered the wine was gone."

Maddox studied his brother. Those were the most words he'd ever heard Naughton string together at one time. Was it because he'd rehearsed what he'd say if Maddox questioned him?

"By the time I got to the vineyards, it was close to seven, and that's when I sent you the text. Where the hell's this comin' from?"

"Why'd you come back to the ranch?"

Naughton mumbled something Maddox didn't catch.

"What was that?"

"I said I should just beat the shit outta you right now for questionin' me like this."

"Just answer me, Naughton. Why'd you come back to the ranch?"

"You didn't answer my text."

"So?"

"*I was worried, asshole.* With all the shit goin' on, I was worried." Naughton was grasping the back of his neck, just like he and the rest of his brothers did.

Maddox hated that he thought it was because Naughton was lying. Just as he was about to call him out on it, Naughton turned around.

"We lost Kade. We thought we lost Brodie, and I couldn't stand the thought of losing you. I called you. I called Alex. I even called Ma. Nobody answered. I couldn't get shit done, so I drove back to the ranch. You think that makes me a pussy?"

Maddox shook his head. That explained why he'd been pounding on the door and yelled for him to open it. "I'm sorry, Naught."

His brother nodded. "What else you wanna know?"

"How'd you know about the safe deposit box?"

"Kade told me about it."

"Why didn't you tell me?"

"About what?"

"That. The land. All of it."

"I answered that question already."

"Answer it again."

"I told you, it's the way Kade wanted it. It wasn't up to me."

"What if the situations were reversed? Wouldn't you have wanted me to tell you?"

"*No, dammit!* Not if you told me that Kade told you not to."

"Why?"

Naughton walked away, but Maddox caught up to him.

"How'd you get here?"

"I drove."

"What?"

"My truck! What the fuck, Maddox?"

"Why were you at Demetria earlier?"

"You're kidding, right?"

"No. I saw your truck parked in the woods, and you were nowhere to be found. Why?"

Naughton shook his head and studied Maddox. "I wish I knew where all this shit was coming from."

"I said it before, just answer the question."

"You know I was at Demetria earlier because you and I asked Brodie to meet us there. After we told him about Kade and Lena, you saw me walk away. My truck wasn't parked in the woods; it was parked right next to yours."

"Not then. Tonight."

"I wasn't at Demetria tonight."

"I saw your truck."

"Bullshit." Naughton walked away again. "Maybe it's a good thing you're here at the hospital, because I think you're losing your damn mind."

"You say your truck's here? Let's go look at it."

Naughton shrugged and kept walking. Maddox followed. The parking garage was lit well enough that when they walked up to Naught's truck, the mud and dirt on the tires and sides of it was apparent.

When they got closer, Maddox ran his hand over it. "This is fresh, Naught, so I'll ask you again. What were you doing there?"

"I wasn't there, Mad."

Maddox bent over and put his hands on his knees. His biggest problem was that he believed Naughton, which meant there was a hell of a lot happening and no explanation for any of it.

"Tell me why Kade asked you not to tell me about the land."

Naught's hand rubbed the back of his neck, and he walked away only to turn around and walk back.

"He said we'd know when to tell you."

"How?"

"When he knew you'd be ready for it."

"How would he know, Naught? Kade is dead."

"He said I'd know."

"How would you know?" Maddox was ready to strangle his brother.

"Alex."

"What about Alex?"

"When you finally realized you were in love with her."

Naughton opened the tailgate and sat on it. Maddox joined him. They sat in silence for twenty minutes or longer before Maddox spoke again.

"What if I never realized I loved her?"

"He knew you would."

"But what if I didn't? Love her, I mean."

Naughton shook his head. "You and Alex were the only people in the valley who didn't know how you felt about each other."

Maddox still had unanswered questions, like why Naught's truck was at Demetria tonight, and what else Lena was hiding. The first question bothered him more than the one about Lena did. Whatever she was running from was none of his damn business.

He looked at his phone and realized he'd been talking to Naughton for more than an hour. He hoped Alex was asleep and not waiting for him to come back.

"Is that why I got the two-hundred acres with the house?"

Naughton nodded.

"What about you?"

"What about me?"

"Kade pulling your puppet strings too? He got somethin' up his sleeve to make sure you end up with the love of your life? What about Ainsley?"

Naughton smiled. "Kade was so full of shit sometimes."

Epilogue

"Just a couple more steps, and I'll take the blindfold off."

"Okay, but hurry up."

Maddox let Alex see the winery, but told her he was blindfolding her before he took her to the next buildings. It hadn't been easy to maneuver her over the cobblestone in the courtyard, especially since he skipped the second building, and the walk was longer. She was being a good sport about it, though, uncharacteristically.

"We're here?" she asked when he opened the massive wooden entry doors.

"Yep, just take a step over the threshold."

"Wait." Alex took a step back.

"What?"

"Aren't you supposed to carry me over the threshold?"

"Aren't we supposed to be married first?"

Alex crossed her arms. "I think we qualify for the common law thing, don't you?"

Maddox laughed, picked her up, and carried her inside. He still hadn't been upstairs, but at least it would be clean the first time they both saw it. Maddox had hired a cleaning crew to come in and get it ready for Alex to see. It had taken two days before it passed Naughton's inspection. He'd even had a new mattress and bedding delivered, and put in the master bedroom, so Maddox and Alex could spend the night here tonight.

"If you don't like the bed," Naught told him, "I'll take it. It's a lot more comfortable than mine."

Maddox asked if he'd slept on it.

"Hell no, but I had to try them out before I picked one, didn't I?"

"Ready?" Maddox asked.

"If you don't take this blindfold off me in the next ten seconds—"

"Go ahead."

Maddox wanted to see the moment she opened her eyes and saw their new home.

"Oh…wow…" she gasped, putting her palms on her cheeks. "Maddox, it's so beautiful. It's beyond—"

"Your most vivid dreams?"

"Yeah, exactly."

"That's what Kade said in his letter to me. It'll be beyond your most vivid dreams."

Keep reading for a sneak peek at the next book in the Butler Ranch Series— *Naughton's Secret!*

He's a text-book loner.
They call him quiet and powerful.
She calls him chauvinistic and conceited.
We call him Naughton Butler.

Naughton Butler refuses to ever bring harm or heartache to his family, so he prefers a life of solitude. But when he and his brother inherit prime vineyard property, Naughton is forced to open up and hire a new winemaker—someone who can handle the job. But the infamous Bradley St. John is nothing like he imagined.

She's a sexy, smart spitfire. Now, Naughton is burdened with his desire for Bradley and his need to protect his family from secrets that could destroy them. With the truth looming, will Bradley realize that there is only one man skilled and strong enough for her: Naughton Butler?

1

Naughton got out of the truck, nodded at her aunt and uncle, and approached her, holding out his hand. Instead of shaking it, Bradley folded her arms in front of her.

"Why are you here?" she asked.

"Evidently I owe you an apology," he said, quietly enough that only she could hear him.

Bradley took a step back. Naughton was a little too heart-stoppingly good-looking to be standing so close to her. "Nice apology. Wait, you didn't actually apologize, did you?" she smirked.

"I'm sorry, Bradley," he whispered, taking another step forward.

God, his voice. It wasn't just his rockin' hard body, but his voice was sexier than all get-out too.

"Forgive me?"

Bradley hadn't moved, but Naughton had. The step forward he took brought him close enough that she could smell the vineyard on him. She breathed in and instinctively closed her eyes. The vines had a certain smell that lingered on the clothes of someone who spent their day in them. It was like the smell of a campfire to those who loved to camp.

"Bradley, I asked you a question." It came out almost like a growl, but a damn sexy one.

"Yeah," she muttered. Why had the fight she had in her only moments ago abandoned her?

"Can we begin again?"

She nodded, still unable to find her voice.

"Good. How about we walk?"

Instead of turning around, Naughton went forward, and Bradley followed.

"Mad says you're the new rock star."

"Is that what he said?"

"No, but I thought you might take it the wrong way if I told you he said you were gonna be the hottest new winemaker on the central coast."

Bradley smiled. At least he was trying to be nice, however misguided his attempt was. "I give credit for whatever I know to my uncle."

"Where'd you go to school?"

"Cornell."

Naughton raised his eyebrows.

"My father lives on the east coast."

He nodded. "And your mother?"

"My mother passed away when I was twelve."

"I see. I'm sorry I asked."

"Jean is my mom's sister."

"Why'd she name you Bradley?"

Interesting that Naughton asked why her mother named her Bradley, instead of her father, or both her parents.

"It was her maiden name."

"No brothers?"

"No siblings."

"I like it."

"What? My name?"

"Yeah."

They walked in silence through her uncle's vineyards, the ones she'd walked every summer of her life, since she was five years old.

"What do you think of Butler Ranch wines?"

"They're good…"

"But not as good as your uncle's."

"Not even close."

He stopped, shook his head, and studied her. "I like you, St. John."

I kept walking.

"Hey, hold up."

I glanced over my shoulder. "What?"

"That's the part where you're supposed to say you like me too. If you want the job that is."

I stopped but didn't turn all the way around. "Yours isn't the only offer I've gotten, Butler. And if me getting the job is dependent upon me liking you, I'd say our negotiations just came to and end."

"Like? Hell, I may have just fallen in love," I heard him mutter as I walked away.

About the Author

USA Today and Amazon Top 15 Bestselling Author Heather Slade writes shamelessly sexy, edge-of-your seat romantic suspense.

She gave herself the gift of writing a book for her own birthday one year. Fifty-plus books later (and counting), she's having the time of her life.

The women Slade writes are self-confident, strong, with wills of their own, and hearts as big as the Colorado sky. The men are sublimely sexy, seductive alphas who rise to the challenge of capturing the sweet soul of a woman whose heart they'll hold in the palm of their hand forever. Add in a couple of neck-snapping twists and turns, a page-turning mystery, and a swoon-worthy HEA, and you'll be holding one of her books in your hands.

She loves to hear from my readers. You can contact her at heather@heatherslade.com

To keep up with her latest news and releases, please visit her website at www.heatherslade.com to sign up for her newsletter.

MORE FROM AUTHOR HEATHER SLADE